She loved this man, now and forever

"If I do not take you to my bed very soon," Alvaro said softly, "I will surely become loco—and you, too, I think."

Lynette flushed as his words evoked sensual images of their lovemaking, and she wondered if he would be irritated by her inexperience.

"Yes," he muttered harshly, mistaking her fear of the unknown for revulsion. "It is a terrible thing that I should wish to make love to the *afianzada* of my own brother."

"No!" she cried. "You don't understand...."

"Alas, I do." He sighed deeply. "I am surely too old to be turned from the path of family duty by nothing more than a pretty face."

As her fingers fumbled with her buttons, Lyn's dazed mind could hardly bear to contemplate the truth that all he felt for her was desire.

Books by Mary Lyons

HARLEQUIN PRESENTS

625—THE PASSIONATE ESCAPE
673—CARIBBEAN CONFUSION
701—DESIRE IN THE DESERT
714—SPANISH SERENADE
763—DANGEROUS STUNT

These books may be available at your local bookseller.

Don't miss any of our special offers. Write to us at the following address for information on our newest releases.

Harlequin Reader Service
P.O. Box 52040, Phoenix, AZ   85072-2040
Canadian address: P.O. Box 2800, Postal Station A,
5170 Yonge St., Willowdale, Ont.   M2N 6J3

MARY LYONS

dangerous stunt

Harlequin Books

TORONTO • NEW YORK • LONDON
AMSTERDAM • PARIS • SYDNEY • HAMBURG
STOCKHOLM • ATHENS • TOKYO • MILAN

FOR JACQUI, Mary, Elizabeth, Lesley and Karen.
In grateful appreciation of all their encouragement,
advice...and patience!

And, after all, what is a lie? 'Tis but the truth in
masquerade.

Don Juan
Lord Byron

Harlequin Presents first edition February 1985
ISBN 0-373-10763-3

Original hardcover edition published in 1984
by Mills & Boon Limited

CHAPTER ONE

'COME back here you little hell-cat!'

Jake's voice echoed in the still desert air as Lynette Harris ran swiftly across the hard parched earth towards the mountainous rocks ahead. Glancing furtively over her shoulder at the knot of men and horses, she saw that Jake was running towards his horse—and his rifle.

'Jeez boss, that dame's taking our gold!'

Taking no notice of his companion's shout, Jake lifted the rifle to his shoulder in one smooth movement, calmly sighting along the barrel at the slim, slight figure of the girl.

'Stop, or I'll shoot!'

Ignoring Jake's command, Lyn hitched up her long skirts as she began to scramble over the outlying large stones, her movements hampered by the heavy leather satchel slung over her shoulder.

Beginning to climb, she quickly dodged behind a rocky pillar as a whining noise and the hard smack of a bullet a foot away warned her of Jake's serious intent. Lyn could hear her own laboured breathing, the heavy pounding of her heart as she drove her tired, weary body on upwards, her feet slipping and sliding over the hard, granite surface of the rocks. Sweat ran down her face, the thin, almost transparent blouse clinging to her damp body as perspiration trickled down between the high peaks of her breasts.

For a moment her mind went blank. The fierce Mexican sun was so hot, burning down on her neck and back as she searched for a foothold, that it was hard to concentrate on what she had to do.

The crack of another bullet only inches away from her face, and the rhythmic thud of Jake's boots as he threw away his rifle and ran towards her brandishing his revolver, brought Lyn swiftly back to reality; reality and fear.

That last shot was far too close for comfort, she warned herself, trying to ignore her almost animal response of sheer panic as she forged on upwards towards the rugged, rocky shelf which hung out over a valley on the other side of the mountain.

As a salvo of bullets whistled about her climbing figure, Lyn tried to shut her mind to the danger, reminding herself that Jake was an expert marksman. It was a thought that brought little comfort to ease her aching, tired muscles as they protested at what she was demanding of her body. Or, to be more precise, what Larry Wilde the director of this benighted film was demanding, she thought grimly. Larry, who saw himself as a second John Ford, was insisting on his conception of reality and 'reality' in this case meant that they were on their sixth take of the afternoon, and those were real bullets that Jake was firing!

Wincing with pain as her foot slipped and she struck her shin on a jagged piece of rock, Lyn glanced upwards. The rocky shelf seemed as far away as ever, and she wished with all her heart that she had never agreed to be Marilyn Thorne's stand-in and stunt girl for this film; a production which had proved to be a disaster from the moment they had set foot in Mexico.

The location shots had taken much longer than scheduled, partly because of Larry's drive for perfection, but also because of a series of accidents to the filming equipment which had held up shooting for days. Then, to cap it all, half the film crew including Marilyn Thorne, the star of the western, had fallen a victim to Montezuma's revenge. This form of gastric upset, which had kept the young star confined to her room for weeks, was a well-known hazard of life for foreigners in Mexico, and aptly named after the Aztec leader who had been so treacherously betrayed and slain by the Spanish conquistadors.

By the end of the second week, when Larry had been tearing his hair out with frustration, it was decided, after long phone calls to the film's backers in New York, that Lyn should take over Marilyn's role on location, doing everything other than close-up shots.

As Larry had explained: 'You're a dead ringer for Marilyn, kid. Same height, shape, face—everything. Right down to her big blue eyes and that long blonde hair. You'll do fine, Lynette, just fine,' he pronounced, sticking a large cigar between his thin slit of a mouth.

Appalled at the suggestion, Lyn had protested vigorously, pointing out that the whole scheme was doomed to disaster.

'It's a crazy idea! We only bear a slight resemblance to one another and my English accent will be a dead give away almost immediately,' she gestured helplessly. 'Not to mention the important fact that I haven't the first idea how to act.'

'Neither does Marilyn!' Larry had snapped before doubling her salary, reassuring her that he would take care of everything, and instructing her to report for make-up at six o'clock the next morning.

It was only the realisation of just how useful the extra money would be in helping to pay the nursing bills for Uncle Charley, and the horses eating their heads off on the ranch back in California, which persuaded Lyn to agree to Larry's mad suggestion that she should impersonate Marilyn Thorne. The beautiful young star, clinging to the comfort of her bed in the small hotel rented by the film company, had also begged Lyn to take her place.

'Lynette, honey, I feel like I'm gonna die,' Marilyn had whispered, looking pale faced and woebegone, blinking away the tears from her large blue eyes as she struggled to sit up in her bed.

It wasn't until yesterday, after six long exhausting weeks, that Lyn had realised just how wrong Larry had been. Marilyn had proved to be a great actress, giving the Oscar-winning performance of her life as she lay pain stricken in her bedroom each morning and night.

Larry had announced an unexpected change in the schedule, sending Lyn back to the hotel where she found Marilyn, not in bed, but downstairs playing poker and drinking tequila with some of the locals.

'Land sakes, Lynette! Surely to goodness you can't blame me for wanting to get away from all that sand and dirt? Cummon honey, sit down and take the weight off your feet and we'll have a nice, cold drink, hmm?'

Lyn hadn't been able to do more than stare at her with weary exhaustion, before doing as Marilyn suggested. She knew she ought to protest, or report the facts to Larry, but she felt too bone-weary, too drained in mind and body to do more than lie back in her wicker chair and pray for deliverance. Deliverance from the everlasting sand, the flies, the burning sun which beat down remorselessly day after day, and above all, to be released from the shouts and bad temper of Larry Wilde who had shown no patience with her inexperience in his pursuit of perfection.

Slowly sipping her drink, Lyn had tried to comfort herself with the thought that they only had one day's shooting left. Admittedly it was the toughest action yet, calling for her to climb up the rocky mountain with bullets whistling around her head, and then the leap off the rocky ledge into the deep valley far below. Only in reality, of course, she would be leaping into a net which had been strategically placed below the ridge to break her fall. She and Larry had argued constantly during the past days about the stunt. Lyn claiming that the net should be higher, while Larry insisted on the longest possible drop to achieve the maximum visual impact. Lyn still didn't feel happy about her leap off the mountain. It was by far the most dangerous stunt she had been called upon to perform, and if anything should go wrong. . . .

A piece of stone slicing across her hand as it ricocheted off the rock face in front of her, jerked Lyn's wandering thoughts sharply back to the present. With a muffled groan as the small wound on her hand began to sting painfully, she saw with relief that there was only a few feet left to climb. Hearing Jake's heavy breathing as he closed the distance between them, adrenalin seemed to sweep through her veins, giving her tired body a fresh impetus as with a final, desperate spurt she gained the flat ledge.

As called for in the script, she glanced back in fear and trepidation at her pursuer, before turning to look out over the valley far below. Time seemed to stand still, her glazed eyes noting the two camera positions on either side of her and sensing, although it was out of her sight, that the third cameraman was aiming his zoon lens up towards her from his ledge far down the mountain. Knowing that she had to wait until Jake was almost upon her and acting as never before, she took her last, despairing glance at the wide blue azure sky, the birds whirling above her head, and the vast panorama of the desert plain which lay spread out before her tired eyes.

She could hear Jake grunting with exertion as he scrambled up on to the ledge behind her, a sharp, metallic clang as his revolver knocked against a rock breaking into the eerie silence.

'You ain't goin' no further!' Jake growled as he walked slowly towards her trembling figure. 'So just hand me that gold like a good little girl, huh?'

It was her cue. With a cry of defiance, Lyn threw the heavy satchel at Jake's tall figure and taking a deep breath she turned and launched herself over the edge of the cliff.

Spinning through the air at 120 feet per second, Lyn felt a blind surge of desperate terror as she realised the net was far lower down the mountain than she had expected it to be. Larry! *Larry must have had it lowered yesterday afternoon when he had sent her back to the hotel!* The net seemed to be rushing towards her with incredible speed as she vainly tried to arrange her limbs in the correct position. She was falling too fast! Much too fast. . . . Surely it wouldn't be able to hold her. . . .

The ropes seemed to slice across her skin as she hit the net, her ears ringing with her own despairing cry and a sickening rumble followed by a snap as one of the retaining guy ropes broke away under the impact of her body. Almost in slow motion her cold, numb hands tried to grasp some of the netting, her fingers tearing blindly at the rope as she felt herself sliding over the edge of the dangling net to fall helplessly down into the valley below. Slipping into a dark infinity . . . falling . . . falling . . . falling.

It was a sound, the high, shrill piping of a bird somewhere nearby that first penetrated the deep mists of darkness. As Lyn's eyelids flickered and slowly opened, she found herself staring uncomprehendingly up at a white ceiling. Trying to move her head, she groaned as a sharp pain like an electric current zigzagged through her brain.

Lyn's low moan brought an instant reaction. She heard the sound of a chair scraping on a stone floor, and a whispering rustle as a figure covered in white draperies materialised beside her.

To Lyn's dazed mind it seemed as if everywhere she looked, her eyes met the reflected glare of brilliant white: the ceiling, the walls of what seemed to be a small room, even her bed cover echoed the pristine, clear neutral colour, dazzling in the harsh sunlight which streamed in through an open window.

'I must be in heaven,' she thought in confusion, not realising until she heard the oddly hoarse and unfamiliar whispering voice, that she had spoken aloud.

'Heaven? *Ah no, señorita.*' The face of a woman, seemingly surrounded by a white cloud, smiled gently down at her. 'This is a hospital. You have been very sick, very ill for many days. Rest quietly now while I go to tell *el medico* that you have awoken.'

With another sweet smile the figure turned to walk over to a door at the side of the room, and only then did Lyn see that her 'angel' was obviously a nun dressed in loose flowing robes.

A furrow creased Lyn's brow as she tried to think why she should be in a hospital. The nun had said something about her being here for many days. How long was that? And then, as she tried to raise her left arm to look at her wristwatch, she found that she couldn't. A heavy weight seemed to be pressing her arm down to the bed, while further investigation showed a similar weight imprisoning her right leg.

Her heart began to thump in her chest, a rushing stream of fright and panic coursing through her prone body. Taking a deep breath to call for help, she almost blacked out at the searing, sharp pain around her chest which resulted from such a simple action.

Lyn was still gasping in agony, helpless even to brush aside the weak tears which filled her eyes as a small, plump man in a white coat bustled into the room, closely followed by the nun.

'Ah, señorita. I am so happy to hear that you have regained consciousness. So happy!'

'What ... what am I doing here?' Once again that strange hoarse whisper seemed to be coming from her throat, a timbre so completely different from her normally light tone of voice.

'Alas, my dear Miss Thorne. What a tragedy! That such a lovely, young and famous film star should have such an accident—*que barbaro!* How dreadful! However, Señor Larry Wilde, your famous director has explained all to me, so you can rest easy. *Si?*'

The doctor's heavy accent made it difficult for Lyn to understand exactly what he was saying. Her ribs felt as though they were on fire and every breath was becoming an effort as she tried to puzzle out why he had called her Miss Thorne? That was Marilyn's name, wasn't it? She probably hadn't heard him correctly, and anyway, just at the moment she felt too ill to bother to query his mistake.

'I—I can't lift my arm or my leg,' she whispered in agitation.

'Believe me—there is no need to worry,' the doctor earnestly assured her. 'Yes, you have broken your left arm and your right ankle, but that is all. Also, of course, you have cracked a few of your ribs, but they will mend very quickly. We are only concerned at the concussion you have experienced, you understand? You have been unconscious for many days, and we must do some tests later to make sure you have suffered no damage in your brain.'

'My voice . . . my voice sounds odd. . . .'

The doctor smiled. 'That is no problem, you have merely been burnt by a rope which crushed your throat.' He bent down to pull aside a bandage around her neck. 'Yes, it is healing well. No problem. You will soon be able to talk to your *afianzado*—your fiancé. I understand that he is very worried.'

'My fiancé . . .?' Lyn's blue eyes widened as she stared at the doctor in dazed incomprehension. Maybe she hadn't heard him correctly. 'Fiancé? Do you mean someone . . . someone that I'm supposed to be going to marry . . .?' She gasped as her cracked ribs once more made themselves felt.

'*Si, si!* Don Felipe has been telephoning this hospital from New York every day. He has been very worried and upset, naturally. How happy he will be to hear that you are now conscious once again.'

'But . . . but doctor, I have no fiancé—none at all!'

Glancing sadly at the nun, the doctor shook his head and muttered something in Spanish.

'There is no need to worry, my dear Miss Thorne. It is just that you have experienced severe concussion. Such a loss of memory is quite usual—very normal indeed.'

'But . . . but I'm not Miss Thorne and I don't have a fiancé!' Lyn cried hysterically, clutching the doctor's sleeve with her good hand in a desperate attempt to make him understand his error.

'Now, now, my dear. You must calm down and rest. You have been saved by the Good Lord from the very jaws of death, and it will take some time for your amnesia to clear. There is nothing for you to worry about, nothing at all. The good sister here will give you some medicine to ease your pain and help you sleep. I will see you in a few days' time and you will find that you are back to your old self again. *Si?*'

It was suddenly all too much for Lyn to cope with. Every inch of her body seemed to be aching, and to continue to protest at what was obviously a simple mistake required more strength and resolution than she possessed at the moment.

Two weeks later, Lyn was, as the doctor had promised, feeling much better. She had begun to get used to the heavy casts on her arm and her leg, and by now her cracked ribs were mending well. It was only her occasional throbbing headaches, together with his patient's difficulty in recalling her true identity, that was causing the doctor some concern.

For her part, Lyn had ceased bothering to protest that she wasn't Marilyn Thorne, and that she certainly

wasn't going to marry Don Felipe—whoever he was—
or anyone else for that matter. Every effort to try and
convince the doctor that she'd never been engaged, and
certainly had never heard of the gentleman in question,
seemed to bring on one of the blinding headaches which
left her feeling sick and confused. It was far simpler just
to lie back and admire the vases full of red roses which
arrived every day from her mysterious, so-called fiancé.

Lyn was convinced that a simple mistake had been
made, one that was obviously due to her substitution
for Marilyn Thorne during the making of the film.
Clearly her best course of action was to get well and
leave this hospital as soon as possible. Nobody had, as
yet, mentioned the matter of payment for her medical
treatment. However, such services were horrendously
expensive the world over; even thinking about the
money needed to pay Uncle Charley's nurses was
enough to make her head start throbbing again. All
good reasons for her to leave the explanations until
later, and in the meantime to lie back and concentrate
on regaining her normally excellent health.

Apart from the doctor's mistaken conviction as to
her real identity, he had been a font of information
regarding the accident. It was through him that she
began to piece together the story of her remarkable
escape from certain death.

'I can remember standing on the ledge ready to jump
into the net, but nothing after that.'

The doctor sighed and shook his head. 'It was clearly
a dangerous enterprise, especially for such a lovely
young girl.'

Not such a lovely young girl, Lyn thought gloomily,
remembering the first glimpse she had been allowed of
herself last week in the mirror. A black eye which had
been turning into a particularly revolting shade of
yellowish-purple, and a gash on her cheek which she
was convinced would leave her scarred for life. All in

all, she had felt that she was a perfect candidate for any producer auditioning for a horror film! She hadn't been in a hurry to look in the mirror again.

'I understand that when your body struck the net, the force was such as to pull away one of the restraining ropes, and the net ceased to be a basket and became a curtain,' the doctor explained. 'As you slid down the rope towards the rocks in the valley below, your foot became entangled in the netting.'

'Is—is that why my ankle is broken . . .?'

'*Sí, sí.* The tangled net held you firmly by the ankle. However, it seems that the force of your descent meant that the net waved back and forth. . . .' The doctor waggled his hands in an effort to communicate a swinging action.

'That is how you came to break your arm, you understand. Your body was banged hard against the rocks of the mountain, cracking some of your ribs and hitting your head. *Sí*—you are very lucky to be alive. It was a difficult rescue I am told.'

Later, as she lay dozing, the afternoon sun's rays casting golden patterns on the white ceiling, she tried to think why the knowledge that she had escaped such a particularly horrifying death didn't seem to mean anything. Possibly dicing with death every time she had performed a daring stunt, or riding bareback in Uncle Charley's circus had inured her to such danger; but maybe it was, as the doctor had said, a matter of delayed shock.

Drowsily Lyn wondered why no one from the film unit had been in to see her. Possibly they were waiting for the 'all clear' from the doctor. Not that she felt up to facing anyone at the moment, but it would be nice to see a friendly face. . . .

Opening her eyes, she realised that she must have slept for some time. The bright rays of the sun had disappeared, their place being taken by the deep reddish glow of sunset. Lyn gave a small sigh as she tried to ease her bruised body into a more comfortable position; a sound that prompted movement from the far side of the dimly lit room.

'Who—who is it? Who's there . . .?' She whispered fearfully in the hoarse voice that she had now come to recognise as her own, her eyes widening as a tall, dark figure emerged from the shadow of the wall and walked slowly towards her.

The man stood looking down at her, his body seeming immensely tall and threatening as he towered over her prone, frightened figure. Her first overriding impression in the dim evening light was of a leashed force, of fiercely controlled anger in the darkly tanned face staring so arrogantly down at her, before he turned silently away to switch on the lamps.

A second glance at the stranger's arrogant, aquiline profile did nothing to dispel his physical aura of spine-chilling menace as he turned to regard the girl lying in the hospital bed. However, the dark, heavy lidded eyes were now empty of all expression as he viewed the cloud of long, sun-bleached honey blonde hair surrounding her pale, frightened face.

He was tall, far taller than most men, his hair as black as night and worn slightly long, curling over the pure silk collar of his immaculate white shirt. Everything about the man, from his expensively hand-tailored lightweight suit, to the heavy gold signet ring on his little finger and the discreet glint of the diamonds on his Rolex Oyster watch, clearly visible as he adjusted her lamp, shrieked of wealth and privilege. What on earth was such a man doing here in the small hospital? And why was he here in her room?

'I can see that the doctor is, *unfortunately*, quite right. You have indeed regained consciousness, hmm?'

His perfect English was clipped and cool, only a faint accent underlying the dark tones of his voice betrayed his Latin American origin.

'Who ... who are you?' she murmured, her body trembling as she sensed the angry turmoil beneath the stranger's cool, calm exterior. Why? Why should this tall, broad-shouldered and autocratic figure be projecting such a hidden force of rage and fury? Why should he consider it 'unfortunate' that she had regained consciousness? Lyn had never seen him before in her life, but all her instincts seemed suddenly sharpened by an overwhelming sense of imminent danger.

The man didn't bother to reply to her tentative question. Turning away to regard the vases of red roses, his finger contemptuously flicked one of the cards attached to a long stem.

'Felipe has been busy, I see!'

Lyn flinched at the heavy contempt and sarcasm underlying his words.

'Are you ...?' Her voice died away. How stupid of her! No, of course he wasn't Felipe, who the moment he had come into the room would have known who she was—or rather, who she wasn't. But if this man wasn't her mysterious fiancé, who was he?

'Am I ... who?' He raised an eyebrow in sardonic mockery, his cynical dark eyes flicking over her pale, bruised face.

'For your information, Miss Thorne, I am Felipe's elder brother. More importantly, I am the head of my family, and I must tell you straight away that I have absolutely no intention of allowing my brother's life to be ruined by marrying a *puta*, a woman such as yourself!'

Lyn gasped, stunned into silence as his cynical eyes swept slowly over her figure lightly covered by the thin sheet. She could feel her face flush with embarrassment at the openly sexual and contemptuous glint in his dark eyes.

How dare he! How dare he talk and look at her in such a way? She didn't know much Spanish, but during all those weeks on location she had picked up a smattering of words from the male members of the film crew, and even she knew that *puta* was the Spanish name for a prostitute!

'You're wrong! You—you simply don't understand. It's all a mistake. . . .' she began, only too well aware of the uncontrollable wobble in her breathlessly hoarse voice.

'Unfortunately, I understand only too well! Believe me if there has been any mistake it is the one you have made, Miss Thorne,' he retorted curtly, walking over to the door and pausing with his hand on the handle.

'I freely acknowledge that at present my brother is quite clearly besotted by you, a woman who regularly displays her charms for all to see. Your last film was quite explicit, was it not? And please . . .' he raised his hand as she opened her mouth to angrily refute his allegations, 'please do not bother to defend your conduct on the basis of that well-known cliché; that discarding your clothes is merely an expression of your belief in your "art"!'

Shaking with rage, Lyn struggled to sit up as his harsh, cruelly contemptuous laughter rang around the small room.

'H-how . . . how d-dare you speak to me l-like this!' she spluttered angrily. 'I don't know—or care—who you are, but you can just get the hell out of here, right this minute!'

Lyn fell back on her pillows, gasping with fury as the blood pounded loudly in her head. The fact that she wasn't Marilyn, as he supposed, seemed completely immaterial at the moment. Whatever Marilyn had done in the past, nothing could possibly justify this man's rude, disparaging words, delivered in such an infuriatingly arrogant and supercilious manner.

'I am only too willing to "get the hell" out of your room as you so elegantly put it!' The dangerous, silky purr in his dark voice sent shivers of apprehension fluttering down her spine as she glared defiantly back at him. 'However, I wish you to clearly understand that I intend to do everything in my power, which is very considerable, to ensure that you never marry Felipe.'

'For God's sake! Why can't you understand that I have no intention of marrying your rotten brother!' Lyn wailed, almost weeping with fury and frustration as, without another word, the door clicked shut behind his departing figure.

CHAPTER TWO

THE next morning Lyn contemplated her breakfast tray with distaste. Normally she enjoyed the *huevos rancheros*, the fried eggs served on top of a tortilla and covered with a red chilli sauce, provided by the hospital each morning. But not today. She was still feeling far too angry and disturbed by the previous evening's encounter with Felipe's brother to face any food at all. As she reached instead towards her cup of coffee, she noticed with dismay that her hand was trembling nervously.

That . . . that man! Never in all her life had she been treated with such chilling contempt, such an autocratic, humiliating disdain. How dare he? How dare he treat anyone, let alone herself, as if they were less than nothing? It was as if he regarded her as of no more account than an insect, which he would dismissively crush into oblivion with a slight movement of his well-shod foot.

Sipping the hot liquid, Lyn fumed with an overwhelming longing to somehow hit back at the stranger. What wouldn't she give to be able to repeat yesterday's encounter, only this time she wouldn't have been so taken by surprise. This time she would be able to tell him exactly what she thought of someone so insufferably proud and arrogant and . . . and so insultingly rude!

Lyn could feel the heat rising through her body, her face flushing as she remembered the way his dark eyes had raked her slim figure beneath the sheets. It was no good, she'd have to clear up the matter of the hospital authorities' mistaken assumption that she was Marilyn

Thorne as soon as possible. She certainly wasn't prepared to have another visit from any more of the mysterious Felipe's relatives—not if they were going to treat her the way his older brother had done! Only . . . only how was she to do so?

On her return to consciousness, she discovered that she had been taken to the hospital with no clothes of her own and, more disturbingly, that her handbag was missing. Thus, there was no way she could brandish her passport or other papers to substantiate her claim that she wasn't Marilyn. Since none of her colleagues on the film had been to see her, she couldn't get hold of her passport, and trying to get a message out of the hospital was fraught with difficulty; among the staff only the doctor and the nun had a smattering of English. She didn't even have any money for a telephone call to the nearest British or American consulate, she realised with dismay. What on earth was she to do?

Sunk in unhappy contemplation, Lyn's mind was too full of her depressing situation to notice the light tap on her door. It was only the sound of high heels on the stone floor which caused her to look up as someone entered the room.

For a moment she stared uncomprehendingly at the dark-haired girl who was grinning so familiarly at her, before she realised it was Marilyn Thorne, who seemed for some unknown reason to be wearing a short, dark wig.

'What on earth . . .?'

'Hush!' Marilyn put a finger to her lips, cautioning silence as she looked back fearfully at the closed door. 'You gotta keep quiet, Lynette. I don't want anyone to know that I'm here.'

'Why ever not?' Lyn found herself echoing Marilyn's stage whisper.

'My agent says I'm not to rock the boat, that's why.' Marilyn came over and perched on the end of the bed.

'Your agent? And what on earth are you doing in that dreadful wig?'

'You're so right! Black hair wouldn't suit me at all. Still,' she sighed, 'that's the way the cookie crumbles at the moment, so I guess I'll have to put up with it.'

'I don't understand what you're talking about,' Lyn looked at the young film star in bewilderment.

Fishing inside her large handbag, Marilyn pulled out some newspaper cuttings. 'I'm talking about you and I being famous, honey!' she laughed softly, leaning forward and placing the newsprint in front of Lyn. 'Great publicity, huh?'

Lyn wasn't listening, her blue eyes opening wide as she viewed the top clipping from the *News*, Mexico's main daily English-language newspaper.

FILM STAR SURVIVES DEATH LEAP screamed the headlines. Rapidly Lyn scanned the report written over a week ago, which stated that Marilyn Thorne, the beautiful young Hollywood film star, had insisted on doing her own dangerous stunts for her new film, and was now lying unconscious and close to death.

Hurriedly, hampered by the fact that her left arm was encased in plaster, Lyn flicked over the other press cuttings.

Vista, the Sunday edition of the *News* had nothing further to add to the first report, but the overseas editions of the *New York Times* and the *Los Angeles Times* both carried prominent coverage of Marilyn's tragic, but brave decision to do her own stunts. The American girl was reported as having emerged from her initial coma, but the papers could give no further details, since they had been barred from the private clinic in Mexico City where she was receiving intensive medication and care.

Lyn's dazed mind seemed to be refusing to function. 'It's . . . it's all. . . .'

'It's all great publicity, that's what it is, honey!'

Marilyn beamed happily, not noticing the bemusement and shock in Lyn's face. 'My agent is absolutely over the moon, simply thrilled to bits! He's already had a lot of calls from magazines wanting my story, and offers of really great film parts for me are just pouring into his office. It's all just so wonderful, Lynette honey, it really is!'

Shaking her head in confusion at Marilyn's euphoria, Lyn tried to make sense of what she had read.

'I . . . I simply don't understand any of this. Why . . . why do all the papers say that it's you who did the stunt; and what's all this about "a private clinic in Mexico City?" I thought I was in a small hospital at San Juan del Rio—not far from where we had been filming.'

'So you are, silly. Only when they hauled you up off that terrible, terrible net,' Marilyn shivered dramatically, 'the guys who rescued you and rushed you here to the nearest hospital thought you were me, right? And that's when Larry had this really great idea.'

'Great idea . . .?' Lyn gazed at Marilyn feeling more and more like Alice in Wonderland every minute. Nothing the film star had said seemed to be making any sense at all.

'Look, even if I can't stand the guy—and God knows I think he's the pits!—I sure have to admit that Larry's smart. We'd finished shooting and all the film was in the can, right? And the people here, in this crummy hospital, are busy thinking that you are me, right? So, that's when Larry put the whole scheme together. OK?'

'For God's sake!' Lyn groaned. 'No, it's not "OK"— I still haven't a clue what you're talking about!'

Marilyn giggled. 'Gee—and I'm the one who's supposed to be so dumb! Larry said that it would be really great publicity, and help sell the film, if everyone continued to think that it was me who had been saved from the jaws of death. So, he fixed everything with my agent, who by the way tells Larry he thinks it's a great idea—a real gas! And meanwhile, the rest of the guys on the film are sworn to secrecy, or whatever. The money men in New York are real happy, and Larry sends everyone back to the US while he flies down to Mexico City and comes to an arrangement with the clinic, so that they will pretend I'm there. Geddit?'

'Oh yes, I "geddit". But . . . but what about me, for heaven's sake?' Lyn protested angrily. 'I've been stuck here seeing no one, I. . . .'

'Not so loud, honey!' Marilyn cautioned. 'Now, there's absolutely no need for you to worry, Lynette, that's what I've come to tell you. First of all, Larry said to tell you that everything's been taken care of. All the hospital bills will be paid by the film company, and they're willing to give you an extra bonus of fifty thousand dollars if you keep your mouth shut. Not bad, huh?'

Lyn fell back on her pillows, feeling totally exhausted as she tried to assimilate all that Marilyn had said. At least she now knew why none of her friends on the film had been to see her and, despite her annoyance at being treated like a piece of flotsam, she had been involved long enough with the film world to see that Larry's scheme was a Godsend, as far as publicity for the film and Marilyn's starring role was concerned. Despite Larry's pretensions, he was very much a second-rate director of what had quite obviously been a medium grade picture. Providing the film company issued the movie fast enough, the public could be counted on to come along in droves to see Marilyn's death-defying leap off the rocky ledge. Everyone's prospects would improve immeasurably—not to mention the film making a lot of money for its backers.

'What do you think, huh?' Marilyn looked at her anxiously.

Lyn shrugged wearily. 'It doesn't look as if I have

much choice, does it?' At least the extra money would take care of Uncle Charley's nursing bills for the next six months, she told herself, and that was one load off her back. Thinking about her uncle prompted her next thought.

'I'm obviously going to be stuck here for some time, Marilyn, but I'm worried about my uncle. He's an old man who's had a stroke, and although I've arranged for him to be properly looked after, I don't want him to worry if he doesn't hear from me for a bit. Can you get a message to him, telling him that I'm OK?'

'Sure I can.' She took out a notebook and pencil from her handbag. 'You just write down his address and telephone number, and I'll see that he gets the message, no sweat.'

Thanking her lucky stars that it wasn't her right arm that was broken, Lyn began to write down the address as Marilyn got up and wandered around the room.

'I think it's real nice of you to take it all so well, Lynette. I mean, seeing as how you could sue the film company for all your aggravation. Oh God!' she clapped her hand over her mouth in horror. 'If you did, it would all come out, wouldn't it? You won't do that, will you, honey? Please say you won't?'

Lyn sighed as she watched the film star's frightened blue eyes filling with tears. She had already swiftly thought of such a course of action, and she was well aware that the film company must have considered the matter also. However, unless she could come to a quick out-of-court settlement, the matter might drag on for years, and with her uncle's mounting bills, plus having to pay the hands on the ranch, it was a risk she couldn't afford to take. Besides which, she couldn't deliberately wreck Marilyn's career. It hadn't been her idea that Lyn should take her place on location, it had been Larry Wilde's. If Lyn wanted to get even with anyone, it was Larry, who had quite deliberately lowered the net, and so caused the accident. Maybe the ropes would have given way if he'd left the net where it should have been, but that she realised was something she would never know. What she did know, was that Marilyn wasn't in any way to blame for this present charade, and in suing the film company Lyn would damage the star's reputation beyond recall. No one would employ her— or ever forgive her—if the real truth behind the publicity stunt were to be made public.

'No. No, I won't tell anyone, Marilyn, I promise. Although,' she added slowly, 'if my arm and ankle don't heal properly, and I can't manage to earn my living for some time, then the film company may have to give me some more money. You'd better warn them about that.'

'Oh sure, I'll definitely do that,' Marilyn assured her with a deep sigh of relief. Looking around the room she noticed the bowls of flowers. 'Hey, what great roses!' she exclaimed.

'*Roses!* Oh my goodness, how could I possibly have forgotten? Just who is Felipe, for heaven's sake?'

Marilyn's blue eyes grew misty. 'He's just a darling, darling man! I love him to bits, I really do, and we're going to get married just as soon as we can.'

'Well, congratulations and all that. By the way,' Lyn added grimly, 'have you ever met his elder brother?'

'No, I sure haven't! That's one guy I intend to keep well away from. Felipe goes on about him all the time, it's a real drag. It's always, "Alvaro says this" . . . and "Alvaro says that" . . . I sure got tired of hearing about him, especially since Felipe didn't think that his brother would approve of me. Which is why,' she confided. 'I've made real sure that I've kept well away from the guy. I want to make sure that Felipe and I are safely married before he gets to hear about me.'

'Look, I'm sorry to be the bearer of bad news,' Lyn said, 'but to put it bluntly he *has* heard about you. He

came here yesterday to tell me—or you as he thought—
that he's going to do everything he can to stop your
marriage. He seemed to think he could do it, too.'

'His brother came here? To this hospital?' Marilyn
gave a small shriek of dismay. 'You mean to tell me
that the Marquéz actually came here? *Oh my God!*'

'"Oh my God!" is just about the right expression,'
Lyn muttered bitterly. 'He is, without exception, the
most dreadful . . . the most arrogant. . . .' She shook her
head distractedly, unable to think of words which
would adequately describe her feelings about the man
who had invaded her room yesterday afternoon.

'Oh gee, Lynette, what am I going to do?'

Looking at the film star's pale face as she nervously
tried to light a cigarette, Lyn suddenly felt sorry for the
other girl, who despite her beauty and fame now looked
lost and unhappy.

'Well . . . I really don't know. It could be, of course,
that we aren't talking about the same person. He never
said anything about being a—what did you call him—a
Marquéz. Although, to be honest, I don't remember
him telling me his name at all.'

Marilyn sighed. 'Yeah, I reckon it has to be the same
guy, seeing as how Felipe only has one older brother;
well, his step-brother to be exact. They're a really old
family, you know, like the earls and dukes and things
you've got in England, and they have been in Mexico
since God knows when. Felipe says they are descended
from a relation of some guy called Cortés who, as far as
I can gather, smashed the hell out of the poor old boys
who wore those feather cloaks and ran the joint here in
Mexico.'

Well, she supposed that as potted history went, it
really wasn't too bad, if somewhat unusual! Lyn
thought, trying not to giggle at Marilyn's colourful
description of the fall of the Aztec Empire.

'Anyhow,' Marilyn continued, 'Felipe says that his

brother, Don Alvaro, doesn't make a big thing about his title, but I think he sounds a pretty poisonous guy. . . .'

'Oh, he is!' Lyn murmured with feeling. 'Can he really stop you getting married?'

'Oh sure, if Felipe was still living here in Mexico, horrid old Alvaro would probably be able to bust us up. Mexicans are really into the "family thing", you know. And Don Alvaro's a really big shot out here, one of the fat cats in the Alfa Group.'

'The what . . .?'

'Oh, you know. . . .'

'Honestly, Marilyn, I haven't the first idea what you're talking about.' Lyn looked at her in puzzlement.

'Well, I just know what Felipe's told me, of course, besides what I've gathered since we've been here in Mexico. It seems that besides all the land they own, the family's money comes from all their various businesses in Monterrey, which is just about the main industrial city in Mexico. Sort of like our Pittsburg,' she explained. 'Anyway, the guys who run things out there—the Alfa Group—are all tied up in a really tight network. They've got the place really sewn up, politics-wise, money-wise and every other-wise. They're known as the "Rockefellers of Mexico" and Don Alvaro, the Marquéz de Costillo y Ramirez, seems to be the richest of the lot!'

'Bully for him,' Lyn murmured sourly.

'Yeah, well, money isn't everything, of course. But it sure goes a long way, Lynette, honey!'

Marilyn lapsed into a gloomy silence as she could plainly see the family millions disappearing from her grasp. And the fact that she might lose Felipe, of course, Lyn chided herself for being so cynical. The American girl seemed genuinely fond of the man she wanted to marry and maybe, given half a chance, they would be very happy together. In any event, she simply couldn't stand being called 'Lynette honey' for one more minute!

'I know my full name is Lynette, but now that we are, well, sort of . . . er . . . partners in crime, won't you call me Lyn?'

'Yeah, Lyn suits you.' Marilyn gave her a sudden smile. 'Want a good laugh? I sure as hell will never forgive you if you tell anyone, but my real name is Doris Evangeline Dubinsky! Ain't it awful? It took me a real long time to get used to being called Marilyn Thorne. That was my agent's idea, and I think it's real classy.'

Lyn laughed. 'It certainly sounds a lot better.'

'Yeah, my agent's really great, I don't know what I'd have done without him, you know. I ran away from home, and was a waitress in a crummy joint, when he came in and said he'd make me a star. Well! I sure as hell had heard that line before, I can tell you! But he was absolutely on the level, and he's looked after me real good ever since. No "hanky-panky" none of that "casting couch" business, if you know what I mean!' She winked. 'He makes damn sure that I don't get bothered by all those smoothie producers and directors who can really spin a girl a yarn. Some of the things I could tell you, they'd turn your hair white—no kidding!'

'I can believe it,' Lyn agreed, having heard rumours about some of the goings on among the Hollywood superstars.

'Yeah, well . . .' Marilyn sighed. 'I wish my agent was keener on the idea of my marrying Felipe, who's a really great guy. I mean, he's so incredibly generous, you know? It's always the best restaurants when I'm out with him, and he can't pass a jewellery store without buying me something real nice. I mean, just look what he gave me the last time I saw him.'

Marilyn waved a slim hand weighed down by a huge

diamond ring, which sparkled in the brilliant sunlight flooding in through the window.

'See what I mean! His family's fabulously wealthy, and so . . . so aristocratic.'

'Well,' Lyn grimaced. 'I hope the rest of the family are nicer than his older brother. He just stood there, looking impossibly arrogant and staring down his aristocratic nose as if I was the lowest of the lowly worms . . . I can't remember when I disliked anyone so much!'

'Gee—I'm sorry Lyn. I guess it's all my fault.'

Lyn frowned. 'What I don't understand is how, if the film company are pretending that you're in a clinic in Mexico City, and Felipe's brother isn't supposed to know of your existence, how it happened that Don Alvaro—or whatever his name is, came here hot-foot yesterday. Because, believe me, he seemed to know all about your film career and the fact that Felipe is crazy about you.'

'Well, I suppose that Felipe must have told him. I had to telephone him as soon as I saw that paper, I really did.' Marilyn looked beseechingly at Lyn. 'I mean, I couldn't leave the poor guy worrying about me, could I? So I told him I was recovering, and also where I really was. I mean, I didn't want him ringing up the clinic in Mexico City and being told I wasn't there, did I?'

'Well, you'd better hope that his brother is the only one he's told about this place, otherwise Larry's "great idea" is going to land us all in trouble, isn't it?'

'Oh gee!' Marilyn's blue eyes widened in dismay. 'I never thought about that.'

If Felipe's as dim as Marilyn, there's a good chance this whole mad scheme will explode in our faces like a time bomb, Lyn thought dispiritedly as she lay back on the pillows and closed her weary eyes. It seemed to have been a long day already, although Marilyn couldn't have been in her room for more than an hour.

'Was Don Alvaro really as horrid as you said?'

Lyn opened her eyes. 'Worse,' she replied succinctly. 'To be frank, I'd honestly advise you to zip up to New York and marry Felipe as quickly as you can—that's if you can face marrying into his family. For my part, I'd want the Atlantic Ocean between myself and that man, and even then I'm not sure that I'd feel too secure!'

'It's a great idea, only ... well, I can't marry anyone at the moment. Not until I get my divorce, that is.'

Divorce! Lyn struggled to sit up in the bed, looking at Marilyn in astonishment.

'Yeah, well, I was just a kid at the time, you know how it is. My agent tells me that this is the perfect opportunity to get a divorce, seeing as how everyone thinks I'm lying in hospital.'

'But ... but you can't just get a divorce that easily, surely?'

'It's all been arranged—I told you my agent was great, didn't I? All I have to do is to take a nice trip to Las Vegas. You see,' Marilyn confided with what Lyn thought was a rather touching, childlike manner, 'I don't think Felipe would be too happy if my husband suddenly turned up out of the blue some day.'

Lyn gasped, her shoulders shaking as hysterical laughter welled up in her throat.

'Are you all right, honey?'

'Yes ... er ... I agree with you that committing bigamy isn't too good an idea!'

'Bigamy?' Marilyn queried, quite obviously never having heard of the word before.

'It means being married to two men at one and the same time, and it's definitely against the law,' Lyn explained, her ribs aching as she tried not to laugh.

'Yeah,' the American girl sighed. 'Like I told you, I've got to get my divorce, seeing that Felipe is expecting to marry a virgin and all.'

'A v-virgin . . .!' Lyn stuttered. 'But . . . but you've been married! I mean. . . .' she blushed.

'For heaven's sake, honey, that's no problem! I'm an actress, aren't I?'

Lyn could feel her mouth opening and shutting like a fish as she gazed speechless at the lovely young star. There was no doubt about it, the whole day had begun to take on a particularly surrealistic aspect. One in which, she thought, it was quite possible that anything could happen. It had been difficult enough to believe that this twenty-one-year-old girl, the same age as herself, had been married and was seeking a divorce. Now it appeared that she was further hoping to pass herself off as purer than the driven snow! For Marilyn's sake, Lyn fervently hoped that Felipe was every bit as besotted as his brother had claimed, otherwise she foresaw trouble ahead for the girl who was blithely humming a tune as she repaired her make-up.

'OK,' Marilyn said as she walked over to study the black wig critically in a mirror on the wall. 'I guess that I'd better get going.'

'What . . . what happens now? To me, I mean,' Lyn queried uneasily.

'You just lie there and get well, honey. It looks from all that plaster that you're going to be here for some time; the doctor told Larry that it will be a good six weeks, maybe more.'

'Yes,' Lyn sighed heavily. 'They haven't told me exactly when my casts can come off.'

'Well, I'll get my nice quiet divorce and then zip back to see that you're OK, before booking myself into the clinic in Mexico City. When he's ready, Larry's going to hold a big press conference, where I'll be brought in on a stretcher looking pale and thankful to be alive. I'm going to give *that* performance all I've got!' she chuckled.

'What am I supposed to do if Felipe telephones or turns up here?'

'Now, don't you worry about that,' Marilyn reassured her. 'He's leaving the family office in New York tomorrow, for a trip to Spain. He was real unhappy about being away for a month, seeing to the family's estates over there, but I told him not to fret. I mean, where could I go if I was incarcerated in this hospital?'

'Fine, just as long as I don't have to see that ghastly Don Alvaro again!'

' *"Gaa-stley"*—I just love your English accent! By the way, that's a really sexy voice you've got all of a sudden. I think I'll try it out for myself.'

All you have to do is get your throat crushed by a rope Lyn thought sourly, and then felt ashamed as Marilyn came over and kissed her lightly on the cheek.

'You've been a real pal about all this mess, honey, and I won't ever forget it. I don't suppose that you're feeling too good worrying about your face and all, but your bruises have almost cleared up.' She stood back to look down at Lyn.

'Yeah,' she added after a moment's scrutiny. 'OK, so I'm pretty and I make the best of what I've got, but you . . . you're really beautiful, and you don't even have any make-up on, for heaven's sake!'

Lyn was too astonished to say anything as Marilyn moved over to open the door. The idea that she could in any way come near to the American girl's loveliness was too far-fetched to even think about.

'Now you just lie back and concentrate on getting well, hmm? Don't worry about a thing, and especially not old Alvaro, OK? Byee . . .!'

Grimacing with pain, Lyn slid down into the bed. Every bone in her body seemed to be aching, almost as painfully as the first day she had regained consciousness after the accident.

Thinking about her talk with Marilyn she realised that maybe she hadn't communicated forcibly enough just what a formidable opponent the girl was taking on in her determination to wed Felipe. Even their brief encounter had convinced Lyn that 'old Alvaro' as Marilyn referred to him, was an extremely dangerous man. Not that he was that old, she thought sleepily. He couldn't be more than thirty-five at the most. It must be his air of ruthless implacability, his commanding stance and overpowering presence which made him appear older than he was. . . .

Totally exhausted, Lyn slept heavily, only waking in time for a late supper, and then falling asleep again. When she awoke early the next morning she felt immeasurably refreshed, and back to her convalescent self again. Having eaten a huge breakfast, she was just brushing her long blonde hair and trying to screw up enough courage to look in the small mirror the nun had placed on the table beside her bed, when there was a loud knock on her door. Looking up, she was astounded to see, not the orderly who was due to remove her tray, but the tall, dominant figure of . . . Alvaro!

'W-what are you d-doing here?' she demanded breathlessly, feeling sick with apprehension as she looked at his formally suited figure whose jacket emphasised the breadth of his shoulders. Her eyes were drawn to the hard set of his wide, thin lips, the frosty glare from beneath the heavy eyelids sharply at variance with his urbane stance as he lounged carelessly against the open door.

'Go away and leave me alone!' Her husky whisper trembled in the air between them, the knuckles of her right hand whitening with tension as she gripped the handle of her brush.

'If I had my own way, I can think of nothing I would like better,' he ground out through clenched teeth, a muscle beating rapidly in his jaw. 'Unfortunately, my brother's urgent plea that our family should take care of you has been listened to by my stepmother, and I cannot prevail upon her to change her mind.'

He turned and imperiously clicked his fingers. Immediately two uniformed men wheeled in a light-weight steel framework on which lay a canvas stretcher.

'W-what's going on?' Lyn cried in fright. 'What's happening?'

'My stepmother is offering you the shelter and comfort of our home,' he snapped curtly, the raw force of his personality becoming evident as he issued rapid instructions in Spanish to the two men.

As they moved towards the bed, Lyn could feel herself losing all control, crying out with terror as she clung with her good hand to the iron frame of the bed.

'I won't go with you! I won't ... I won't ... Help! Please help me, someone ...' she called out as loudly as her injured throat would allow.

'Por Dios!' Swearing violently under his breath, Alvaro strode forward, quickly unclasping her fingers and sweeping up her shaking figure in one smooth movement. His eyes narrowed as for a long moment he stared down at the trembling girl in his arms, before he spun on his heel and placed her surprisingly gently down on the stretcher, quickly covering her white hospital shift with a blanket.

'Leave me alone ... please let me go ...!' she cried, sobs shaking her slight body. 'I'm not Marilyn Thorne, really I'm not. It's all a terrible, terrible mistake!'

Seemingly deaf to her pleas, Alvaro clicked his fingers again and she felt the trolley move out of the room and down the corridor.

'Ah, Excellency. If I could just have your signature. For our records, you understand.'

'Doctor!' Lyn cried out, suddenly swept by an enormous feeling of relief. 'You won't let him take me away, will you?' she tried to raise herself on the stretcher as she recognised the doctor's voice. 'I—I don't want to leave this hospital,' she begged, weak tears of fright and shock blinding her for a moment as she caught hold of the doctor's white coat.

'Ah now, señorita. Be calm. You will be well looked after, believe me. His Excellency, here, has assured me that you will have the very best medical care. As you know, I have been very worried about your amnesia. . . .'

'I don't have amnesia!' she shouted huskily, almost choking with frustration and fear. 'I'm not Marilyn Thorne. My name's Lynette Harris, and this man . . . this man is abducting me!'

'There, there . . .' the doctor murmured, patting her hand as he spoke softly in Spanish to Alvaro. 'You must go now, little one. All will be well,' he added, gently pulling away his white coat from her desperate fingers.

'For God's sake, tell Marilyn . . . tell Larry Wilde what's happened,' she called out desperately as the trolley began to move once again.

Falling back exhausted, she realised that it was no good trying to make anyone understand. There was no one here in this hospital who believed a word she was saying. No one who was in a position to gainsay Alvaro as his minions lifted the stretcher into a low ambulance, closing the doors with a bang before going around and getting into the front seats.

Lyn could see very little, only enough to be certain that Alvaro wasn't in the ambulance as it sped through the streets of the small town, and on over increasingly bumpy roads out into the countryside.

When at last the vehicle halted, Lyn's body was trembling so hard that she could hear her teeth chattering in her head. What was going to happen to her? It was possible to believe anything of Alvaro— simply anything. Did he intend to kill her, thus removing her irritating presence from his brother's orbit? He had said that he was taking her to his stepmother's home, but that could be just a subterfuge, she thought hysterically, just an excuse to remove her from the hospital. The panic-stricken thoughts ran like frightened mice hither and thither in her brain as she waited in fear and trembling to know her fate.

With a sudden rush of air, the back of the ambulance was opened and the stretcher on which she lay was slid out. Looking up, she saw Alvaro's tanned face leaning over her, his lips cruelly twisted into a cynical, sardonic smile.

'Well now, señorita,' he drawled softly, raising his hand above his head. 'This is as far as you go. . . .'

Lyn didn't hear any more, as with the complete conviction that he was going to kill her, something seemed to snap in her brain. The world began to revolve faster and faster as it seemed that she was being drawn into a deep, bottomless pit of everlasting darkness.

CHAPTER THREE

THE fiery red ball of the dying sun was beginning to sink slowly behind the far mountain peaks, the tall cypress trees which surrounded the large swimming pool area casting shadows across the sparkling blue water, and over the slight figure lying on a reclining chair.

Putting down the book she had been reading, Lyn sighed as the faint sound of a church bell rang from far down the valley. It was her favourite time of day, here at the *hacienda*, when the late afternoon lengthened into the dusk of early evening, and soft breezes carried the scent of the pine trees from where they grew on the distant slopes of the Sierra Madre.

Glancing at the heavy plaster encasing her left arm, Lyn recalled the specialist's promise of its removal in a week's time. He had, however, refused to commit himself to a definite date for her release from the cast on her ankle. She was forced to console herself with the thought that with the use of both her arms, she could at last hope to manoeuvre herself about on crutches, and not have to rely on assistance from the bewildering army of servants at the *hacienda*, as she had been forced to do during the past three weeks.

As she looked about her at the calm, serene tranquillity of her present surroundings, it seemed almost incredible that it was only three weeks since she had been forcibly dragged from the hospital in San Juan del Rio. It was equally impossible to believe that she had been in such fear of her life, that she had fainted on being removed from the ambulance out on to what she now knew to have been a small airstrip in the desert.

Slowly surfacing from the swirling dark mists which had engulfed her, her ears had seemed to be filled by an unfamiliar, distant hum. It had taken her dazed mind some minutes to comprehend that she was lying on the soft cushions of a couch in what was, she realised, the body of a private jet aeroplane. Turning her head sideways Lyn looked down the aisle of the cabin towards an open door through which she glimpsed the back view of a uniformed pilot seated at the controls. Her vision was suddenly obscured by the tall figure of Alvaro, his broad-shouldered body seeming to dominate the enclosed space. She was unable to prevent a small cry escaping her lips, closing her eyes in fright as he sat down on the couch beside her.

Expecting she knew not what, she was startled by the touch of his fingers gently brushing away the hair from her forehead, followed by the cool relief of a wet cloth being applied to her fevered brow. Lyn's eyelids fluttered open, gazing mesmerised at the tanned face of Alvaro, as he bent over her prone, trembling body. She could see the glint of silver strands among the dark hairs of his temple, the sensual curve of his lower lip as he smiled down at the frightened girl. A smile, she noted, that did not reach the dark hooded eyes regarding her so intently.

Lyn felt a quiver of impotent helplessness run through her body, a depressing sense of futility at her puny efforts to defy this man. He appeared so arrogant, so invincible, so completely the master of his fate.

'It is regrettable that you should have been so frightened,' Alvaro murmured softly. 'But surely you can see that it is pointless of you to attempt to defy my wishes, hmm?'

She could feel her cheeks flame as his words so accurately echoed her unspoken thoughts, unable to tear her eyes away from his face as his low, mocking laugh rang like a knell in her ears.

'Where—where are you taking me?' she whispered huskily as she felt his hand slide slowly down her head to toy with a tendril of her long blonde hair.

'Surely I explained the matter to you back at the hospital?'

'But I don't understand. . . .'

Alvaro's jaw tightened, his features suddenly taking on a frightening stern expression. 'It would seem that my stepmother is concerned that Felipe's *novia*-to-be should have all the care and attention possible. She has insisted that you are to be taken to our *estancia*, our home in the mountains above Monterrey, where you can be properly nursed back to health.'

'I was being perfectly well looked after in the hospital,' she retorted coldly. How dare Alvaro just bundle her up like a parcel, merely to satisfy a whim of his stepmother?

'Yes, I freely admit that I have failed, in this instance, to persuade Felipe's mother to any other course of action. It is a regrettable error on her part,' he shrugged. 'But not, I feel, an unsurmountable one.'

Lyn's eyes blinked as she registered the fact that there seemed to be at least one person who refused to be pushed around by this hateful man. However, the thought of having to meet Felipe's mother and having to pretend to be someone she wasn't, was of no comfort.

'But I don't want to have anything to do with your family!' she protested angrily.

'No?' His lips twisted into a sardonic smile. 'Surely intending to marry my brother must involve you with our family, hmm?'

Opening her mouth to deny any interest in Felipe, she suddenly realised that in doing so she would be breaking her promise to Marilyn. She already felt ashamed of having done so back at the hospital, her blind terror at being kidnapped having driven all other considerations from her mind. However, Alvaro was completely convinced that she was Marilyn, and until she could devise some method of escape, she would be forced to continue the masquerade.

Besides, even if she did manage to convince this arrogant man that she wasn't who he thought, it could only have dire consequences for poor Marilyn and the unknown Felipe. What little she knew of Alvaro was enough for her to be certain that he would immediately move heaven and earth, both to trace the young film star and then mercilessly expose Marilyn's part in the publicity stunt. Desperate as she felt her position to be, Lyn simply couldn't face the thought of Marilyn's wrecked career lying on her conscience.

'*Ah ya!* I can see that you have decided to be sensible and stop pretending that you are suffering from amnesia!' Alvaro's shoulders shook with cynical amusement. 'As an actress you are obviously talented enough to convince the good doctor in the hospital. However, trying to fool a specialist from Mexico City would be another matter, would it not? I am glad to see that we can dispense with the services of such an expert. It would merely have embarrassed my family, since we both know just what sort of a woman you are!'

Lyn glared at him with loathing, his cruel jibe bringing the hot colour flooding back into her face.

'You know absolutely nothing about me,' she retorted bitterly, infuriated by his mocking smile.

'But yes,' he purred silkily, clearly enjoying her suppressed rage and anger at his words. 'You are like so many loose women who will do anything to capture a man, especially a man who is foolish enough to provide them with the creature comforts of a luxurious life. Would you have looked at Felipe if he had not been wealthy? I think not, señorita! It is clear that your manifold charms are for sale to the highest bidder, and. . . .'

Without conscious thought and provoked beyond reason, Lyn raised her hand to wipe away the cynical and contemptuous sneer from his arrogant features. But she had forgotten that it was enclosed by the heavy plaster cast. The sound of the dull thud as it cracked against his high cheek bone sent a stream of sick apprehension and self disgust coursing through her body.

The shock she experienced at her action, so totally at variance with her normal behaviour, was reflected by Alvaro. The blood seemed to drain from his face, leaving only the vivid red mark of her blow. His dark eyes flashed with a fury that was terrifying in its intensity.

'*Jess!*' He swore violently under his breath, an arm snaking out to lift her trembling body towards him, his other hand grasping a handful of her long hair at the back of her head. A choking sob broke from her lips at the hard pressure as he crushed her against his chest, tears springing into her eyes as he sharply tugged her hair downwards, exposing the long arch of her neck and tilting her face up towards him.

'No one, *but no one*, strikes the Marqúz de Costillo y Ramírez. . . . No one, you understand?' he snarled, his eyes blazing with an unleashed anger as he stared down at her, his face only inches from her own.

'L-let . . . let me go . . . she gasped, trying to twist her head from side to side, before something in his eyes triggered a primeval response deep within her body and she ceased struggling, her panting breath sounding like thunder in her ears as she felt all her resistance suddenly drain away.

'*Por Dios! Dios!*' she heard him swear under his breath and then the hard pressure of his lips possessed hers with ruthless savagery. There was no way she could avoid the cruel punishment as his mouth bruised hers, the relentless pressure forcing her lips apart and allowing him to ravage the softness within.

It wasn't a kiss, it was a determinedly malevolent assault as his mouth and tongue began a lustful exploration, a punishing invasion of her shattered senses. It was grimly humiliating and hateful, and yet she was powerless to control a knot of excitement, deep in her stomach, which flared through her shaking figure. She seemed unable to exert any control over her weak, exhausted body, or still the quivering softness of her lips as they trembled beneath his. As if in immediate answer to her response, he abruptly let her fall back on the cushions.

'*Vaya!*' he muttered, his hooded eyes raking her pale face and nervously fluttering eyelids with fastidious contempt. 'That I should so forget what is due to my family by even touching such as you! *Es increible*, no?'

'You ... you're disgusting ...!' Lyn gasped, weak with shock. Her bruised mouth was burning, her body trembling and aching with an unfamiliar pain.

'Am I?' he drawled mockingly. 'Then I suggest, señorita, that you are very careful not to provoke me in the future!'

The grim menace of his words hung in the air between them as he rose and without a backward glance strode towards the front of the aeroplane to sit down beside the pilot.

Left on her own, Lyn was a prey to a mass of conflicting emotions, the principle one being of deep hatred and loathing of the man who had just exercised such a deeply disturbing physical assault on her senses. Alvaro had determinedly forced her to become aware of himself as a man, in a fashion that she had never experienced before. In forcing her to submit, both to his superior strength and also to the powerful, erotic sensuality he had engendered, he had roused dormant emotions she hadn't known she possessed, and destroyed all her innocent illusions at one and the same time. She would never be the same person she had been before, and for that she would never forgive him—*never!*

The aeroplane banked sharply and presently she felt the pressure in her ear drums which warned her that they were descending towards their destination. Turning her head to glance across the cabin, she saw that the windows of the aircraft were filled with swirling puffs of cloud, which dissolved every now and then to reveal the harsh granite formation of mountainous peaks. It was obvious that they were going to crash, flying so close that she could see fissures in the rocks. Mentally and physically exhausted by the day's events and Alvaro's recent assault on her senses, Lyn could only apathetically welcome a final solution to her problems. Shutting her eyes she waited for her approaching end, only to hear the whining rumble of wheels being electronically lowered, and then the rough bumps as the aircraft landed on the flight path.

The aeroplane came to a rest and Alvaro walked back down the aisle, completely ignoring her nervous figure on the couch. The door of the aircraft was opened, and he ran swiftly down the steps and out of her sight. Minutes later, evidence of his organising ability was forcibly demonstrated as two white-coated attendants entered the plane and eased her body on to a stretcher before carrying her carefully out and across the tarmac to a waiting ambulance.

During her transfer from the jet, Lyn determinedly kept her eyelids firmly shut. There was no way she was prepared to allow Alvaro to glimpse the weak, hopeless tears of misery which welled up in her wide blue eyes, despite all her efforts to control her emotions. I won't give him the satisfaction, she told herself grimly, only too clearly able to imagine his scornful, mocking expression at her weakness.

She was so absorbed by her unhappy thoughts that

she hardly noticed when the ambulance began to move, only to be jerked out of her reverie moments later as the vehicle halted and the rear doors were opened. Bewildered, she tried to sit up and see what was happening, a sharp tug at the stretcher causing her to fall back on the pillow as she found herself being carried once more across the tarmac of a runway, coming to a halt beside a red helicopter, beside which stood Alvaro's tall, forbidding figure. He directed the attendants to hoist her stretcher up into the helicopter, following behind and moving forwards as she was placed across a bench seat at the rear of the plane.

Never having flown in a private jet before, let alone a helicopter, Lyn realised with a lump of depression that her whole existence seemed to have been turned upside down since Alvaro had invaded her life. With dull eyes she watched as he stripped off his jacket and seated himself at the controls. His thin white silk shirt emphasised the breadth of his shoulders, tightening across his back to display his powerful muscles as he leaned forward to flick a switch. Putting on sunglasses, which made him even more of a darkly threatening figure, she saw that he was indeed intending to fly the helicopter as he clamped earphones on over his head.

The deafening noise of the rotor blades beginning to whirl filled the small cabin with their pounding, rhythmic drone as with a lurch the helicopter rose into the sky. Lyn tried to still the lump of apprehensive depression which seemed to lie like a large stone in her stomach. Where they were going and what was going to happen to her, were questions to which she had no answer.

Fifteen minutes later they had arrived, Alvaro putting the helicopter down as gently as thistledown. The door was rolled back and a chattering group of servants were directed to remove her stretcher.

I'm just like that child's game of 'pass the parcel',

Lyn thought almost hysterically, feeling extraordinarily lightheaded as she saw that they had landed on the wide green sward of a plateau in the mountains. The fresh, spring-like air seemed curiously thin. Her damaged ribs ached as she tried breathlessly to fill her lungs while she was being gently placed in the back of an open landrover.

Tossing a bunch of keys to a young servant, Alvaro jumped into the back of the vehicle beside her. Viewing her laboured breathing he gave the nearest approximation to a genuine smile that she had seen so far.

'It is the altitude,' he explained. 'We are high up in the Sierra Madre, very different from the desert which surrounded the hospital. You will soon get used to it.'

Lyn didn't reply as she concentrated on catching each breath and absorbing her surroundings. They passed down a concrete road, past corrals containing horses contentedly munching the rich green grass, before drawing up outside an astonishingly large building which looked exactly like a colonial mansion found in the deep south of America.

It all looks more like *Gone with the Wind* than Mexico, she thought, before the facts of her situation and the dreaded imminent meeting with Alvaro's family filled her mind to the exclusion of all else.

With an impulsive, unconscious gesture for help, her right hand caught hold of Alvaro's sleeve as he prepared to leave the vehicle.

'Please ...' she whispered, her large blue eyes wide with apprehension as she gazed at him beseechingly.

Thinking back later, she decided that she must have imagined the softening of his face and the reassuring quick squeeze of his hand, before he leapt to the ground.

His arrival provoked a noisy response. Lyn could hear the barking of dogs and she distinguished the joyful yell of a child amidst the general cacophony of

servants chatting loudly to each other before Alvaro
barked out a command and quiet fell on the assembled
company.

With a few short, sharp statements in Spanish,
Alvaro organised her removal from the vehicle.
Servants wearing the same dark uniform as those which
had met the helicopter lifted her gently down, past the
tall white columns of the wide porch and into the cool,
dark interior of the house.

It took some time for her eyes and ears to adjust to
the general mêlée as smiling faces bent over her,
mouthing various unintelligible Spanish phrases. It
wasn't until she had been transferred along a corridor,
past countless dark portraits on the walls, and was
gently placed on a large, high bed, that she was able to
take stock of her surroundings.

She appeared to be in what must be a bedroom,
although it was larger than the huge sitting room back
at her uncle's ranch in California. On one side of the
long wall was a stone fireplace, ready laid with wood
for cold nights up here in the mountains, and before
which was placed a sofa and two upholstered armchairs
covered in a pale sage green silky material. A deep piled
rug of the same colour covered the honey-coloured
parquet flooring, the walls of the room being hung with
a creamy slub silk, the same colour as the curtains
which moved in the soft breeze from the three open
French windows. They led out into what seemed to be a
wide stone patio set with chairs and tables, while in the
distance she could see the sparkling shimmer of sun on
water.

But what drew her eyes was an enormous crystal
chandelier hanging in the middle of the room, and
whose diamond-cut drops caught the sunlight to send
glinting prisms of light dancing about the ceiling. It was
altogether the most magnificent room she had ever
seen. How Marilyn would love it, she thought suddenly,

before a slight cough attracted her attention. She looked up to see a tall, slim, dark-haired woman of about fifty, dressed in black, smiling gently at her across the room.

'I hope that you will be happy here with our family. It is my great pleasure to bid you welcome to our home, señorita.'

Like Alvaro, the woman spoke in clear, correct English, although with a heavier accent than ... her stepson? Was this Felipe's mother?

Lyn struggled to sit up in the large bed, the woman coming quickly to her aid with a small murmur of concern.

'I am Felipe's mama,' she explained, sitting down on the bed beside Lyn and gently patting the hand which wasn't covered in plaster. 'It has been such a long journey for you, you must be exhausted,' she continued with a warm smile.

'Yes, I ... er ... I am rather tired,' Lyn murmured, feeling not only awkwardly shy, but conscience stricken at having to deceive such an obviously kind woman.

'*Bien*. I will order perhaps an omelette for you, yes? And then you maybe would like to sleep before meeting all the family later on this evening?'

'Yes ... er ... señora, that sounds fine. Although I'm so tired that I'd prefer to leave all food until this evening, if that's all right?'

'Of course.' The woman paused for a moment. 'I would normally be addressed as Doña Elena, but my dear señorita you must call me "mama", since you are soon to marry my son, yes?' She laughed softly at Lyn's blushing cheeks, mistaking the flush of shame for that of girlish modesty.

Doña Elena looked about her, clicking her teeth in annoyance. 'The servants have not brought your luggage. I must see to that immediately.'

'I'm afraid that I don't have any luggage, not even a

toothbrush,' Lyn replied, explaining that she had woken up in the hospital bereft of all belongings and in a white shift, similar to the one she was wearing at the moment.

'You have nothing else to wear? *Por Dios!* You poor girl, I must see what I can do.'

A knock on the door was followed by the entrance of Alvaro's tall figure.

'My son,' Doña Elena turned swiftly towards him. 'Do you realise that this poor girl has nothing to wear, other than this ... this garment. Could you not have provided her with something more suitable?'

'Ah, mama! How could I have done so?' He grinned at his stepmother, his stern features relaxing as he regarded her fondly. 'Besides, think what enjoyment you will have in buying a new wardrobe for the señorita.'

'*Ah, los hombres!* Men!' Doña Elena raised her hands and eyes to heaven. 'Never do they think about a woman's clothes, eh!' She winked at Lyn before directing a stream of Spanish at her stepson.

Lying back on the pillows, Lyn clearly saw that Alvaro and Doña Elena had a fond regard for each other. Perhaps she hasn't seen the other side of him, she thought dully, assailed by waves of exhaustion.

'Ah, you poor girl, you look so weary—so very tired.' Doña Elena stood up. 'I will leave you now to have a good sleep.'

'Please will you call me by the name of Lyn,' she asked as his stepmother moved over to join Alvaro by the door. If she was going to have to stay in this house for any period of time, at least it would be better to be called by her own name. It would be safer too, she thought, dreading the idea of giving herself away by not responding to Marilyn's name.

'Lyn?' Doña Elena looked puzzled.

'Yes ... er ... my friends call me ... er ... Lyn. It's er ... er ... a shortened form of Marilyn,' she improvised wildly, and it wasn't entirely a lie, she consoled herself.

'Ah yes, I see,' Doña Elena nodded. 'Lyn, it shall be. Sleep well my child,' she added, moving past Alvaro and out of the room. He remained, pausing for a moment with his hand on the door knob as if he intended to say something. But Lyn determinedly closed her eyes, blotting out the sight of his tall, aristocratic figure. She had taken just about as much as she could stand from this man—more in fact—and she simply didn't feel capable of coping with his hard, raw personality. The sound of the door slowly closing behind his departing figure was the last sound she heard as she lapsed thankfully into the welcoming arms of a deep sleep.

She was awoken in the early evening by the entrance of Doña Elena, followed by what seemed to be a battalion of servants carrying clothes for the large wardrobes in her room, make-up for the dressing table and toilet requisites which they placed in the adjoining bathroom. Lastly a wheelchair was pushed into the room and set strategically beside her bed.

'I have given the matter some thought,' Felipe's mother announced. 'And I am sure you do not wish to keep looking at those heavy plaster casts all day. Since dresses might be awkward, it occurs to me that trousers would be best for the moment. *Si?*'

'Oh yes! Thank you ... er ... Mama, thank you so much!' Lyn looked with delight at the brilliant cerulean blue silk shirt and trousers being displayed by Doña Elena. She hadn't realised until now just how sick of her hospital shift she had grown, or how much she had missed even the morale-boosting effect of a lipstick. At the sight of so many clothes, bottles of perfume and all the cosmetics she could possibly desire, her eyes shone with overwhelming gratitude for the other woman's thoughtful kindness.

Doña Elena laughed at the sheer hunger reflected in Lyn's face, explaining that the clothes had belonged to her daughter Mercedes when she was a young girl. Now aged twenty-five she was staying at the *hacienda* for a visit with her young son Carlos, aged six. Doña Elena laughed again as she opened her arms to describe Mercedes' plump figure, now no longer slender enough to wear the clothes which had been hanging in the wardrobe of the bedroom she had used as a girl.

'My daughter was so happy to choose these clothes for you, although she cannot, alas, provide you with . . . er . . . with underclothes. However, she has managed to find some of these.' Doña Elena held up a brief pair of pants.

The fact that she didn't have a bra to wear was not likely to be a problem, Lyn thought, thankful that her high, full breasts were firm enough not to require support. And amidst all these beautiful clothes, it was a small matter of no importance.

'I'm so . . . so very grateful for . . . for everything. . . .'

Doña Elena cut her words short with a dismissive gesture as all the servants left the room, except a small dark girl who smiled shyly at Lyn. She was introduced as Maria, Doña Elena explaining that the girl was to be her personal maid and would now help her to get dressed.

Never having had the assistance of a maid, personal or otherwise, Lyn felt nervous as she accepted Maria's help across to the bathroom. However, by the time she was dressed, the silk trouser suit perfectly fitting her slim, slight figure, they had become friendly. It simply hadn't been possible for her to remain on her dignity, not when trying to balance on her good leg while she attempted to pull the trousers on over the other limb encased in plaster!

Laughing together at their combined efforts, Maria helped her into the wheelchair, and moved it across to the dressing table. Looking at herself in the mirror some minutes later, Lyn shrugged resignedly. She had done what she could, but although she had managed to disguise what was left of the bruise around her eye, the gash on her cheek still seemed to be vividly evident, despite Maria's protestations to the contrary.

'*Por favor* . . .' said the girl, taking a brush and drawing it through the long, fine length of Lyn's blonde hair. '*Que hermosa!* So lovely, so beautiful is your hair. . . .'

Maria's halting words were interrupted by a loud knock as Alvaro entered, the maid moving at his direction to stand at the side of the room with lowered eyes.

Lyn looked at her with astonishment, until she recollected the stories she had heard of the proprieties which must be observed between men and women in Spain. Was it the same here in Mexico, she wondered? A friend of hers had been engaged to a Spaniard who had been shocked at the license allowed in America, even between those about to be married. A woman who was seen to have been alone with a man, was apparently considered to be besmirched.

That's rich! Having contemptuously called me every name under the sun, it's surely just a little late for Alvaro to now suddenly remember the niceties of polite behaviour, she thought, grimly viewing his advance towards her with two flat leather boxes in his hands.

'Since you have brought no jewellery with you, my stepmother thought you might feel awkward on meeting the rest of the family,' he said in a hard, curt voice. 'She has directed me to give you these.'

He flicked open the boxes to display a heavily ornate gold necklace and a garniture set of pearls and turquoise, comprising a necklace, brooch and earrings.

'Oh no! I . . . I couldn't. . . .' Lyn gasped, looking in awe at jewellery such as she had never possessed.

Alvaro flicked a finger against the gold necklace. 'It is of no great value,' he pronounced dismissively.

'But I can't possibly accept such . . . such a gift from your family.'

'As Felipe's *afianzada*, you are now regarded as a member of the family,' he pointed out icily. 'For however short a time that may prove to be!'

'You mean, just as long as it takes you to persuade your brother of my unworthiness, I suppose!' she retorted angrily.

'Exactly!' he agreed smoothly, his mouth twisting in a cynically mocking smile.

Looking at his tall, handsome figure clothed in an expensively cut dinner suit, Lyn seethed with a longing to somehow dent the apparently impervious armour of his self-possession, and supercilious arrogance. To punish him for his appalling rudeness and callous disregard of exactly how awkward she felt, having been placed by him in these foreign, alien surroundings. The protection of Maria's presence seemed like a sudden gift from heaven.

'Maybe . . .' she murmured softly, glancing provocatively at him through lowered eye lashes, 'maybe I should tell your stepmother of your plans to come between Felipe and myself.'

'No—you will not!' he commanded sternly.

'Well, I certainly ought to warn Felipe of your intentions. I don't think he will be very pleased to know just how you assaulted me on the aeroplane, do you?'

'*Jesús!* You vixen!' A muscle clenched in his jaw, beating angrily against the taut skin. 'I will not permit you to do so!'

'Oh yes?' She gave a low laugh, which even to her ears sounded husky and uncertain, echoing the uneven pounding of her heart. 'Just try and stop me!' she taunted.

'With pleasure!' he ground out savagely, moving

menacingly towards her until a startled movement from Maria recalled the maid's presence to his mind.

Lyn flinched, fear feathering down her spine at the grim fury in his flashing dark eyes. What on earth had possessed her to incite his wrath in this way? She knew that she had no intention of saying anything to Doña Elena, and Felipe was out of the country, and therefore unobtainable. How could she be so insane as to be tempting fate like this?

'Now is not the time to discuss this matter further,' he ground out through clenched teeth, his dark eyes sweeping over the nervous figure of Maria. 'However, be very sure that if you dare to challenge me, señorita, then you are indeed a cretinous fool!'

The ferocity in the softly snarled words echoed in her ears long after Alvaro had spun on his heels and left the room, slamming the door loudly behind him.

CHAPTER FOUR

'*Tía* Lyn. *Tía* Lyn . . .!' The high-pitched, excited voice of Mercedes' small son Carlos, as he ran into the large swimming pool area, broke into her thoughts and brought her sharply back to the present.

'Look, I can do it, I really can. Watch me!'

Lyn smiled as the six-year-old boy came to a halt by her chair, concentrating hard as he began to toss three tennis balls into the air, one after another. He managed to juggle them for a few moments before he missed a catch and they fell to the ground.

'Well done!' she laughed, clapping her hands in applause as she assured him that with more practice he would undoubtedly become a good juggler.

'Good enough to join your uncle's circus?' he asked breathlessly.

With a sinking heart, she regretted ever having mentioned the circus to the small boy. He was an amusing, lively child who was obviously somewhat lonely up here at the *hacienda*, far away from the friends of his own age back at his home in Mexico City, and Lyn's arrival had provided him with a captive audience. A fact that was literally true, she thought wryly, her mobility being severely limited by her plaster casts.

During the past weeks, when he wasn't riding his small pony or begging lifts from his uncles, Ramon and Miguel, as they drove about the *estancia*, he had spent most of his time by her side. They had become good friends and to amuse him, and herself, she had played innumerable games of Monopoly, taught him card tricks and how to juggle and, desperate for inspiration one day, she had told him stories of circus life. Lyn had immediately realised her mistake when Carlos had shown that he found the subject fascinating, demanding more and more stories. She had only reluctantly complied, after making him promise that he wouldn't tell the other members of his family. Lyn didn't know anything about Marilyn's background, but she was almost certain that the film star had never been a bareback rider! Any mention of her circus background would be bound to expose the masquerade she had been laboriously maintaining during her stay with Alvaro's family.

'Now, Carlos, you know that we decided that the circus was to be a secret between us,' she warned him. 'Grown ups don't ... er ... don't always approve of such things, you know. Besides, I told you that my uncle had disbanded his circus two years ago.'

'Sí, sí, I remember. I won't tell anyone,' he promised. 'But only if you will show me how to juggle five balls at once.'

'That's blackmail!' Lyn smiled at his wickedly grinning face. 'Well, I'll probably drop them since it's a bit hard to do it sitting down. Still, here goes!'

Taking the balls from Carlos, and after a few false starts, when she found she had not allowed for the weight of the plaster cast on her arm, she began to throw the balls into the air in a swift rotating circle. Encouraged by the excited shouts of the small boy, she was concentrating so hard that she didn't hear the firm footsteps approaching. It was only when a shadow fell across her chair that she looked sideways, startled to see the tall figure of Alvaro.

The tennis balls fell from her suddenly nervous fingers to bounce and run away across the stone patio. She'd stayed out here by the pool far too long, she realised, distractedly watching Carlos as he scampered after the tennis balls. Ever since their confrontation in her bedroom on the evening of her arrival, she had taken great care never to be alone in his company. She had always made quite sure that she had the protection of other members of the family, successfully foiling his repeated attempts to hold a private conversation with her.

How could she have been so foolish! She knew that Alvaro always came to the pool at this time of day, relaxing in an early evening swim after his return in the red helicopter from the family's offices in Monterrey. Castigating herself for her folly, she stole a quick glance at the wristwatch she had been lent by Mercedes. She was surprised to see that it wasn't she who was late, but Alvaro who was unaccountably early.

She turned to pick up the slim walkie-talkie set to call for her wheelchair—the brilliant idea of Ramon, Alvaro's youngest brother—and glanced swiftly up through her eye lashes at Alvaro's rigid figure. She may have been startled by his unexpected appearance, but he appeared to be stunned as he gazed down at her in stupefaction.

'Where—where did you learn to juggle like that?' he demanded imperiously.

Instead of being annoyed at his accusatory tone, she could feel her shoulders shaking as a tide of amusement ran through her at the sight of his shocked face. Well, I've certainly managed to surprise Mr Know-All! she thought, and then, unable to contain herself, she let forth a peal of laughter.

He stiffened immediately, the haughty expression of outrage etched on his features causing her increasing mirth.

'If . . . if you could just . . . just see your face!' she gasped, almost doubling up as she was assailed by another paroxysm of laughter.

'I am glad to see that you find me so funny,' he snapped coldly and turned towards Carlos. 'Hey! It is past your bedtime and your mother is waiting to give you your supper. Hurry along now, hmm?'

'*Sí, tío,*' Carlos said meekly as Alvaro bent to give him an affectionate hug. '*Buenos noches, tía Lyn,*' the child added, coming over to place a sticky kiss on her cheek before running off towards the house.

'Have you finished?' he queried sarcastically as she wiped the tears of mirth from her eyes.

'Yes, I . . . I was just going to call for my wheelchair,' she muttered, putting out a hand towards the table beside her reclining chair.

'There is no need,' he murmured, a mocking grin twisting his lips as he picked up the instrument, tossing it lightly in his hand. 'I will take you back myself when I have had my swim, and after . . . er . . . after the few words I wish to have with you.'

Cold, steely fingers of apprehension seemed to grip her throat. 'But I . . . I ought to be getting dressed for dinner. It is Maria's day off and it always takes me much longer on my own . . .' she babbled breathlessly, disturbed by the gleam in his dark eyes.

'Ah, perhaps you should have thought of that before now,' he drawled coolly. 'Especially, before you decided that I was so amusing, hmm?'

'Oh, for heaven's sake!' Gritting her teeth she stretched out her hand for the radio receiver. 'Please give it back to me.'

'I think not. Later, maybe, when I am ready, and only at my convenience.' He turned and began to walk away towards the changing rooms at the other end of the pool.

'You're certainly not being very funny now!' she called out, smouldering with impotent fury. 'Of all the arrogant, obnoxious, Male Chauvinist Pigs I've ever met . . . *you're the tops!*'

His only reply was a derisory bark of dry laughter as he disappeared from her view.

Swearing under her breath, Lyn looked wildly about her for something which would enable her to escape to the sanctuary of her room; but there was nothing! However much she cudgelled her brains for inspiration she knew that she was stuck, effectively marooned out here on the patio with no way of evading the forthcoming confrontation with Alvaro. He had made quite sure of that—damn him!

Leaning back in her chair, Lyn tried to simmer down and control the hard knot of tension which seemed to have her stomach firmly in its grip. OK, so she was a fool to have underestimated Alvaro. However, it was no good lying here fulminating about having been out-manoeuvred by that . . . that dreadful man. Because, in a very few minutes, she was going to have to be clear headed and with all her wits about her, wasn't she?

With a heavy sigh she realised that her present predicament was partly her own fault. During the past three weeks she had grown careless, revelling in the warm, welcoming family atmosphere—something she had never experienced before.

Her nerves had been like coiled springs that first evening as she had been taken in her wheelchair along to the *sala*, where she had found the members of the Costillo family drinking sherry before dinner. Once again, as in her bedroom, the sheer magnificence of the room took her breath away. Huge crystal chandeliers sparkled down on the assembled company, and on the glowing silk of what she later learned was a rare, Aubusson carpet which completely covered the floor of the large room. Ancient antique furniture was mixed with modern sofas and comfortable armchairs, while in the great fireplace logs burned against the slight chill of the April evening.

Confusedly, Lyn tried to sort out what seemed to be a crowd of people to whom she was introduced. It was only when she was half-way through the delicious meal in the equally large dining room, that she began to distinguish one member of the family from another.

Alvaro, as head of the family, sat at the end of the long oval table with the plump, smiling figure of his sister Mercedes on his left. Back in the *sala*, Mercedes had beamed with delight as she saw how well her clothes fitted Lyn. 'And the colour,' she had enthused, admiring Lyn's long, sun-bleached blonde hair, 'so *apta*, so perfect for your colouring, yes?'

Lyn had tried to express her overwhelming thanks, but Mercedes had waved her hands dismissively.

'*De nada!* It is, how do you say, my pleasure to help you. My mother has told me that you arrived with nothing. It must have been so very terrible for you.' Her dark eyes shone with sympathy.

Longing to say that the only thing which was terrible had been Alvaro's behaviour, Lyn realised that she could hardly say as much to his sister, who was beckoning to a slim man on the other side of the room.

'You must meet Ricardo, my husband,' Mercedes announced, introducing Lyn to a handsome man who bowed deeply over her hand.

'Ah, that I should have the great privilege of meeting Señorita Thorne, the famous film star! What a fortunate man Felipe is, how lucky to possess such a jewel!'

Despite his handsome appearance, Lyn had immediately taken an instinctive dislike to Ricardo Diaz. The more so when he tried to flirt with her under the very nose of his wife. She had thought him far too oily and suave, a type that she had met often enough during the two years she had been involved with the film world. Men who traded on their good looks and charm, expecting women to leap into bed with them at the drop of a hat.

Looking now across the table as he chatted to Doña Elena, she saw nothing to reverse her first impression. I bet he's already cheated on his wife, she thought, feeling sorry for Mercedes who had so generously provided Lyn with the clothes she was wearing.

Ricardo was certainly very different from Ramon, Felipe's younger brother who was still at university. Tall and good looking, he had the same upright bearing of Alvaro, only in his case the arrogant, aristocratic lines were absent from his face as he turned to smile at her.

'It must be very exciting to be a film star!'

'No, I'm afraid it isn't,' she answered, his evident admiration boosting her self-confidence amidst the sea of unfamiliar faces. 'In fact, it's extremely hard work!' she added wryly, recalling the heat and discomfort of the recent filming on location.

'But to be such a success, to know that millions have seen your films, it is good, yes?'

Lyn gave what she hoped looked like a modest shrug, and hurriedly sought to change the subject into a safer channel.

'Er ... tell me, Ramon, is that another of your brothers?' She nodded towards a man of about twenty-five with the same tall, good-looking features of Ramon and Alvaro, and who was sitting close to a petite, quiet-looking girl who looked up at that moment and gave Lyn a shy smile.

'Ah yes, that is Miguel. He, and Sanchia who is sitting next to him, have only been married a few months. Miguel runs the *estancia*, you understand, and he and his wife live in a house down the valley.'

'And who is the beautiful woman over there, talking to Alvaro? There wasn't time for me to be introduced before dinner. Is she another one of your sisters?'

'Who, Dolores ...? Ah, no, she is our cousin. Her mother was the sister of Alvaro's mama. My father's first wife died giving Alvaro birth, you understand. It was very sad,' he added as one of the many servants stepped forward to replenish Lyn's glass.

Sipping her wine, Lyn looked at Dolores as she placed a slim, delicate hand on Alvaro's arm. Aged about thirty, the woman was exquisitely dressed in a shimmering silk, wine-coloured gown, which set off to perfection her pale olive skin and sleek black hair drawn into a chignon at the back of her head. Her smooth elegance made Lyn suddenly feel very gauche and unsophisticated.

It had occurred to Lyn that Doña Elena had over-reacted somewhat when she had expressed such horror at Lyn's lack of clothes, make-up and jewellery. Now, as she gazed at the crystal glasses, the solid silver cutlery—and even silver plates for heaven's sake!—comprehension began to dawn. Lyn felt she was beginning to understand that to people as wealthy as those present, the thought of being cold and hungry, of being without the creature comforts of life such as the army of servants, and even the unbelievably large diamonds on Dolores' fingers, for instance; without all these things life would indeed be unimaginable. . . .

'Dolores says that she is staying here with my mama while her *apartamento* in Monterrey is being decorated.' Ramon's voice cut into her thoughts. 'But me,' he winked, 'I think she is here to be near Alvaro!'

'She isn't married?' Lyn looked at him surprised and then cast another glance down the table. Dolores had struck her as an experienced woman of the world, not as a spinster who had reached the age of thirty without being married.

'*Sí*—she was, but her husband has been dead for two years. He was very old, you understand. Oh yes, she would like to marry Alvaro, but,' he shrugged, 'what my brother has decided, I do not know.'

Watching the sleek, sophisticated woman and the sensual hunger of her parted lips as she smiled at Alvaro, there was no doubt in Lyn's mind that they were, or had been, lovers. It was plain to see in her slanting glances, the constant touch of her bejewelled fingers on his arm, the intimate possessive look which declared quite plainly: this man is mine.

And the best of luck! Lyn thought grimly as Alvaro bent his dark, arrogant head towards Dolores. Taking on Alvaro would be like being locked in a cage with a ferocious lion! Unless she had found a way to tame him, that woman was going to need all the luck that was going.

Just at that moment, Doña Elena cleared her throat loudly. 'I do not think, my son, that you have properly welcomed Señorita Thorne to our home.'

His stepmother's faintly reproving words caused a slight flush to stain Alvaro's tanned cheeks, his dark eyes glinting down the table at Lyn.

Get out of that one, buster! was the vulgar thought that flashed through her mind as she sipped the dark red wine, which was producing a satisfactorily soothing effect on her ragged nerves.

'Ah yes,' Alvaro murmured silkily. 'I have been very remiss, have I not. We are all entranced, señorita, to have you in our midst for what must be, alas, such a regrettably short visit.' There was a long silence as he waited for a servant to pour some more wine into his glass. 'Before the señorita marries my brother, Felipe, I meant, of course,' he added smoothly.

Lyn seethed as she registered his veiled threat and caught the underlying sardonic tone in his voice. No one else at the table seemed to have noticed anything amiss in what he had just said, however, as they lifted their glasses in salutation.

He's not going to get away with that! I'll show him two can play at his game, she thought swiftly, as the family waited for her to respond to Alvaro's words.

'I . . . I am so happy to be here, among the family of my beloved Felipe.' She took a deep breath, the amount of wine she had consumed lending her courage

as it flowed through her veins. 'However,' she added, 'I
... er ... I must express my deep appreciation and
gratitude for all *dear* Alvaro's tender, loving care and
consideration.' She lifted her glass towards him, smiling
brilliantly into his face and noting with satisfaction the
flash of anger in his dark eyes, a muscle throbbing in
his clenched jaw.

The effect of her huskily voiced words was not
entirely what she had imagined. The members of the
family smiled their appreciation, but Dolores' smooth
head had jerked up, and she was now directing her far
from friendly eyes in Lyn's direction.

'I am surprised at your voice, señorita,' she said.
'Surely it has changed since your last film, the one
where you ... er ... lost your clothes? Although, of
course,' her laugh tinkled around the room, 'You
remove your clothes in all your films, do you not?'

Taken aback, Lyn could feel a tide of crimson
flooding across her face at the unexpectedly bitchy
assault. What on earth, she wondered, could she have
said to upset Dolores? Confusedly, she tried to pull
herself together as she hunted through her mind for a
reply. To her astonishment, she was rescued by Alvaro.

'The señorita's throat was crushed by a rope during
her terrible accident,' he reproved Dolores coldly.
'Moreover, Felipe has told me that the señorita intends
to give up her career after they marry, and in any case, I
understand that an actress has no choice but to do what
her director tells her.'

Lyn looked at him in amazement. Alvaro, actually
defending the very actions about which he had
spoken with such fastidious disgust? It didn't make
sense!

Ramon, sitting beside her, supplied an answer. 'My
brother is quite right. Whatever has happened in the
past, you are now a member of our family, and it was
very wrong of Dolores to say such things.'

'It . . . it's very . . . er . . . kind of your family to take that attitude,' she murmured.

'I must confess that I have not seen any of your films,' Ramon said. 'However, if what Dolores says is true, I see I must go to the cinema immediately!' He gave her such an outrageously wolfish smile, that Lyn couldn't repress a giggle.

'You're much too young to be allowed into the cinema,' she teased.

'Ah no! I am twenty years of age, and very much a man!'

Lyn tried to hide her smile at the young man's *macho* statement. He was gazing at her with such frank admiration that she realised she must be very careful, not only to make sure she didn't encourage what looked like a dawning infatuation, but at the same time not to be too dismissive as to wound his pride.

'I didn't really mean it,' she assured him, looking up to see Alvaro's dark eyes regarding her with cold disapproval.

Oh—oh! So much for coming to my support. It looks like we are back to the old scenario, she thought wearily, suddenly feeling tired and depressed at Alvaro's continuing hostility.

At a signal from Doña Elena everyone began to leave the table. Lyn, pleading tiredness, was able to make good her escape to her room, but not before she caught a flashing glance of venomous dislike from Dolores.

Although she couldn't think how, she'd obviously made an enemy of the beautiful woman, Lyn thought uneasily as Maria helped her weary body into bed. Well, that would only give Dolores and Alvaro something else in common, wouldn't it. Quite apart from whatever sort of intimate relationship they enjoyed together.

However, the overriding thought in Lyn's mind as she drifted off to sleep that night was that she must, she really must make absolutely sure that she was never alone with Alvaro. He was quite clearly determined to cause her the maximum trouble in his efforts to separate Marilyn from Felipe, and if only for the young film star's sake she must try and frustrate his intentions.

The sound of a splash as Alvaro dived into the swimming pool only served to remind Lyn that although she had been successful in evading Alvaro so far, it looked as if her run of luck was going to end this evening. And where, for that matter, was everyone? In the past weeks, Dolores had, unknowingly, been a great help. She had always appeared in the nick of time to rescue Lyn when it looked as if Alvaro had managed to isolate her from the other members of the family. Now, when Lyn could have done with her bitchy presence, the damn woman was nowhere to be seen!

Determinedly ignoring Alvaro's lithe, deeply tanned body as he forged his way up and down the pool in a fast crawl, Lyn tried to think what he could want to talk about. Marilyn wasn't due to turn up at the hospital for another three weeks at least, so she was certain that he didn't suspect her substitution for the film star.

There had been one or two awkward moments, of course, principally when she couldn't apparently recall details of Marilyn's life and profession. It was always Dolores who, prompted by some evil genius, put her finger unerringly on the weak spots of Lyn's masquerade. She had been reduced to pleading amnesia so often that maybe Alvaro was going to suggest she saw a psychiatrist!

Her distracted thoughts were interrupted as Alvaro climbed out of the pool and began to dry himself briskly with a towel. Darkly tanned skin rippled over the breadth of his shoulders, and his black swimming trunks were brief enough to display a hard, flat stomach over the long length of his tightly muscled thighs.

Her face and body suddenly seemed to be unaccountably hot, and she vividly recalled the punishing force of his embrace in the aeroplane, the hard pressure of his lips on hers. She was still struggling for composure as he shrugged his powerful shoulders into a short, pale blue towelling robe and walked across the patio towards her.

'Well, señorita ...?' he drawled mockingly, half seating himself on the cast iron table, his eyes slowly travelling over her slim, cream silk trousers and matching sleeveless blouse.

'What ... what do you w-want?' she stammered, suddenly feeling as nervous and gauche as a young teenager.

'Merely to speak to you, of course. What else could I possibly have in mind?' he murmured cynically as he extracted a slim gold case from the pocket of his robe and withdrew a thin cheroot, lighting it with a matching gold lighter before placing both objects beside him on the table with unhurried ease.

'I have absolutely no idea!' she snapped nervously, hating him afresh for having trapped her in this invidious position, and with no avenue of escape.

Alvaro exhaled, the smoke forming a perfect ring. 'I have not been ... er ... unaware of your attempts to forestall such a private meeting between us,' he murmured, his eyes gleaming with unconcealed amusement. 'However, I have news of a development about which you may well be interested.'

'Really?' She shrugged as casually as she could, trying to still the flutters of apprehensive dread which tingled down her spine. She felt breathless and stifled by the sheer height and breadth of his powerful frame. As he leant so casually against the table, his stance was reminiscent of that of a wild, dangerous beast—one that was lithe and ready to spring on its prey at any moment.

'Yes, *really*!' he echoed mockingly, clearly enjoying her discomfort. 'I have to tell you, my dear Lyn, that Felipe is far away from here, in Spain.'

'I know that.'

'Ah, but maybe you did not know that I have instructed him to remain there for the next year, hmm?'

Lyn's first reaction was an almost hysterical feeling of relief. If that was all he had to say, she certainly had nothing to worry about! She was just opening her mouth to tell him so, when she suddenly realised that if she did, she would completely give the game away. Marilyn's reaction to the news would be one of heartbreak at being parted from Felipe for so long, wouldn't it? Although why he expected his brother to be so spineless as to accept Alvaro's command, was beyond her.... Hang on! she told herself excitedly. Alvaro had her pinned down here at the *hacienda*, but he didn't have quite the same control over Felipe, surely? The brothers were obviously close, but maybe ... maybe not quite as close as all that ...?

'Telling my darling Felipe to stay in Spain is no big deal!' she declared scornfully in as near an approximation to Marilyn's voice as she could manage. She'd been damn lucky so far that none of the family, being Mexican, seemed to have noticed that her accent wasn't American. She'd have to try and mimic Marilyn's nasal tones from now on, since Alvaro clearly wasn't letting matters slide as she had hoped. In fact, he was even more dangerous than ever.

'For heaven's sake! If darling Felipe can't leave Spain, then I'll just have to go there and join him, won't I?' She flashed Alvaro a brilliant, malicious smile. 'It's not still the days of Columbus, honey. Ever heard of aeroplanes?'

She was pleased with her performance, but on looking up at his deep frown as he studied her intently, she suddenly wasn't quite so sure that she was succeeding in fooling him. Her heart quailed as she realised the only route to safety lay in making him so angry that he wouldn't be able to think clearly.

'Then it would appear that I must find a way of keeping you here, until I have dealt with Felipe, hmm?' he purred silkily.

Trying to ignore the deep pounding of her heart, she raised her chin defiantly. 'Oh yeah? And just how do you think you're going to do that, *smart ass*?'

Oh God! I've done it now, I really have. Lyn flinched as he jumped to his feet, the furious, dark flush of colour beneath his tanned skin echoed by his eyes which became almost black with rage. For one terrible moment she thought he meant to strike her, before he lowered his deep eyelids, hiding all expression as he clearly fought to control his anger.

'I will find a way, believe me!' he snarled at her. 'And don't you *ever* dare to talk to me like that again!'

'Huh—you can dish it out, but you sure can't take it, can you honey?' Lyn continued recklessly, fervently praying that Marilyn would appreciate all that she was doing for her. 'I guess that you're just nothing but a big old cream puff—all gas and wind! And ... er ... and now I'd like you to call for my wheelchair,' she added hurriedly as she glimpsed the blood draining from his face to leave him white and shaking with rage.

Not even giving her a chance to cry out, he swiftly bent to roughly pick her up in his arms. 'You wish to return to your room?' he rasped savagely. '*Sí, con mucho gusto, señorita!* With much pleasure I will take you there, if only to beat the living daylights out of you. *Sí?*'

'Put me down! Put me down this minute!' she cried, her struggles hampered by the heavy casts on her arm and leg as, completely ignoring her, he strode purposefully out of the swimming pool area and towards the open french windows of her bedroom.

Her wildly twisting figure was helpless within his firm grip as he entered the room, walking across the floor to throw her down on to the large bed. She lay winded for a moment, her blue eyes widening in terror as he sat firmly down on the bed beside her.

She was deeply frightened now, realising that in provoking Alvaro she had stepped way outside her league. 'Please ... please go away ...' she whimpered huskily, trembling violently as she saw no relaxation in the stiff, clenched jaw, no release in the dark, hooded eyes from which still flashed angry sparks of rage.

'A cream puff, am I? All gas and wind, eh?' he ground out through clenched teeth, the faint sibilance in his voice investing his words with terrifying menace.

'Please! I'm sorry ... I. ...'

'Too late, señorita,' he hissed. '*Por Dios!* You will pay for what you have said to me today—and I know just how to punish you, do I not?'

'Oh God! No ... no ...!'

Ignoring her despairing cry, he bent over her, burying his hands firmly in her hair either side of her wildly twisting head. There was nothing she could do to avoid the slow, deliberate descent of his tanned face, neither was she able to escape his mouth which possessed hers in the hard, brutal punishment that he had promised.

She tried to fight him, her good arm beating frantically against his body as it pinned her firmly down against the soft mattress. Her struggles became weaker and she realised that she was completely at his mercy, able to offer no defence as he ruthlessly savaged the full softness of her mouth.

Unable to move, she felt as though she was slipping into a dark void of unconsciousness, all thought and reason obliterated by the pressure of his mouth. A pressure that went on and on, ruthlessly demanding her total surrender, until almost imperceptibly, his lips ceased their cruel punishment, as his tongue began an exquisitely sensual exploration of the inner moistness of her mouth, one that was devastating in its effect.

She seemed helpless to resist the answering flame which the soft seduction of his lips ignited within her, a deep wave of heated excitement flooding up through her body. One of his hands moved slowly down over her figure to unbutton her blouse with swift expertise, gently brushing aside the fine silk as his fingers lightly stroked her pale skin. She gave a startled gasp as his hand closed over her full breast, a low husky moan breaking from her throat as he touched its swollen, rosy tip.

The next second she was free. Alvaro had released her and was now standing up beside the bed. Dazedly, her mind and body still locked in pleasure, her breath rough and uneven, Lyn gazed up at him, unable to speak.

His face was flushed, his dark eyes glittering like polished jet, their pupils dilated as he stared unwaveringly down at her. He too seemed to be breathing unsteadily, but, unlike her, he had not lost the power of speech.

'You say you love Felipe? Hah! The way you responded to my embrace, señorita, convincingly proves to me that you do not! However, I know you for what you are, and the trembling sweetness of your lips and body beneath mine means nothing to me—nothing at all! It is *infame* that Felipe should marry such a woman—one who gives herself so freely to any man! And I promise you that he will never do so. *Never!*'

CHAPTER FIVE

ALVARO had gone, the door slamming behind him as Lyn lay stunned on her bed, weak tears escaping from beneath her tightly closed lids. She was so shaken that she couldn't move for several minutes, and when she did manage to persuade her trembling limbs to obey her mind, all she could do was to curl into a tight, miserable ball, too shattered to think properly.

She didn't know what had shaken her most— Alvaro's determined, brutal assault, or her own weak submission to the erotic seduction of his lips. She should have known when she deliberately provoked him, that he would retaliate, although she would never have guessed the form his retaliation would take. Her head ached where he had so firmly grabbed her hair, her mouth throbbing from the fierce pressure of his lips. However, Lyn was less concerned with the aches and pains he had inflicted on her, than with the overwhelmingly sensuous urgency that had filled her entire being as his hand had touched her breast. It was clearly useless to even bother to point out to him that no one had ever touched her in such a way before. He was totally convinced that she was a loose woman who had permitted many men the intimacy of her body.

A crimson tide of shame flowed over her as she recalled that this was the second time he had roused her innocent, dormant emotions. But on this last occasion his touch had triggered an explosion of sensual awareness inside her trembling body, the intensity of which she had never known. How could she have responded so ... so eagerly to someone she didn't even like, someone whom, in fact, she hated with every fibre of her being? That such a man could engender such feelings of raging desire seemed completely inexplicable, and totally outside her experience.

She was still lying on her bed, the dreadful row and its erotic aftermath filling her mind to the exclusion of all else, when Doña Elena knocked on the door and entered her room.

'Are you not joining us for dinner tonight, Lyn?' she asked, looking with concern at the young girl's pale, tear-stained face.

'No, I don't feel very well. . . .' Lyn murmured. 'I think . . . er . . . that maybe the shock of my accident has just suddenly hit me,' she lied in a valiant attempt to deflect any suspicions Alvaro's mother might have as to the real cause of her upset.

'Ah, but yes, that is very understandable,' the older woman murmered, leaving Lyn to feel ashamed at having to dissemble to someone who had been so kind to her. Lyn had never known her mother, but if she had been given a choice, Doña Elena was just the warm, comforting figure she would have hoped to have been blessed with.

'Never mind, my dear. You lie there and I will have a light supper sent in to you, yes? There are only a few of us for dinner, since Alvaro and Dolores have flown down to Monterrey for the evening. That will mean that Mercedes and I will have a chance for a really good gossip! Rest well, my child,' she added, quietly leaving the room.

I bet Alvaro's having a fine old time with dear Dolores, Lyn told herself miserably. There's a couple who *really* deserve each other—I can't think which I dislike most. Maybe Dolores is the sort of woman who likes to be treated the way he assaulted me? Her mind was suddenly filled with visions of Dolores and Alvaro together, a deep, involuntary moan escaping her lips at the thought of the two lovers and their intimate, private life.

A moment later she was sitting bolt upright in the bed, gazing with shocked, blind eyes into the distance as she asked herself the question: why? Why should she care one way or another exactly what those two poisonous people did when they were alone together?

Her tired, exhausted mind eventually found the whole problem far too much to cope with. Easing herself on to the edge of the bed she swung her legs to the floor and stared blindly down at the carpet as she slowly began to remove her clothes and put on her nightgown.

Heavy eyed the next morning, she was sitting in a dressing gown sipping her morning coffee, the toast on her breakfast tray lying untouched before her, when Mercedes put her head around the door.

'May I come in?'

Lyn smiled wanly. 'Yes, yes of course. How is my friend Carlos this morning?'

'Alas, he has not been a good boy. Of course, I had realised that my brother, Alvaro, was in a bad mood, but when Carlos threw a paper dart straight into his uncle's fried egg—*ola* . . .!'

'Oh Lord!' Lyn gave her a guilty look. 'It's all my fault. I taught Carlos how to make paper darts yesterday. Was . . . er . . . was Alvaro very angry?'

'*Sí!* He was shouting and raging, and all the time the dart just stuck there in the egg!' Mercedes' lips began to twitch and a moment later she collapsed into a chair, shaking with laughter.

Despite her general misery, Lyn couldn't help grinning either. 'Never mind, I expect Alvaro will forget about it very soon, he's much too fond of Carlos to remain angry for long.'

'*Dios*, I hope so. He was so nasty to everyone. How do you say it?—like a bear with a sore head. My mama said to keep far away from him this morning.'

'That sounds like excellent advice,' Lyn murmured. If only she had been able to follow it yesterday.

Mercedes frowned. 'It is not like my older brother to be so angry. Now Miguel, yes, he has a quick temper, but Alvaro is always so kind and so calm, you understand.'

Lyn stared at her in astonishment. Alvaro, so kind and calm? Not as far as she was concerned, he wasn't. Granted his sister ought to know him, but ever since Lyn had met the man, she had encountered nothing but unkindness and furious anger. Really, if she wasn't feeling so miserable, she'd be screaming with laughter at Mercedes' view of her brother's character.

Lyn looked up to see that the older girl was wandering aimlessly around the large bedroom, looking at the books on the bedside table before moving slowly over to fiddle with some of the scent bottles on the dressing table. Ever since she had been at the *hacienda*, Mercedes had lapsed into these abstracted moods, looking tense and unhappy. Maybe she's missing her husband, Lyn thought, Ricardo having gone back to Mexico City the day after her arrival.

'I . . . er . . . I wonder if I could talk to you, Lyn? To . . . well, to ask your advice?'

'Yes, sure. What's the problem?'

'It's . . . it's just that I can't talk to Mama or Alvaro. They didn't want me to marry Ricardo in the first place, you see. And now, although they gave in to my wishes, they are sure to be angry and say that they knew it would happen all along.'

'I'm sure they wouldn't, whatever it was,' Lyn said soothingly. Oh dear, it looks as if Ricardo's got involved with another woman, she thought, looking at Mercedes unhappy face. What on earth can I possibly say that will be of any help to her? However, the story related was not at all what she expected.

Stripped down to its bare essentials, it seemed that both Alvaro and Doña Elena had been strongly against the marriage to Ricardo Diaz. He came from an old but

impoverished family and they feared that he was
marrying Mercedes for her money. This, she hotly
denied. So heatedly, in fact, that Lyn guessed it
probably was the truth.

However, as Mercedes explained, her father had just
died at the time, and both her brother and mother
didn't want to be too hard on the young girl who was
then only seventeen. So, Alvaro had persuaded her to
wait a year, and in the meantime had made it very clear to
Ricardo that while Mercedes would have a large dowry,
there was no place for him in the financial set up of the
family. Ricardo had proudly asserted his belief in his
own prospects, spurning the thought of any income
from Alvaro and, a year later, they were married at a
magnificent ceremony in the ancient baroque cathedral
in Monterrey.

'At first, Ricardo worked very hard in a big banking
house in Mexico City,' Mercedes explained. 'But then
for some reason he lost the position, I do not know
why. Although he had many other jobs, he did not stay
in any of them for very long and my dowry was soon
gone. I blame myself, Lyn. You see, I was so busy
having just given birth to Carlos, that I didn't really
notice what was happening.'

Lyn thought Mercedes was being unnecessarily hard
on herself, and that Ricardo was only following the
path of many young men who liked the good life, but
weren't prepared to work for it.

And then, as related by Mercedes, one year ago
Ricardo appeared to have fallen on his feet, at last.
Money, which had once been so tight, suddenly seemed
to be in plentiful supply. Anything Mercedes wanted
she could have, and Ricardo bought himself a large,
flashy car and seemed to be spending money like water.

'He used to work very hard. Always away from home
until late at night. But I was happy and content that he
should be such a success in his work. And then, a

month ago, I began to have strange phone calls. Strange men, *norteamericanos* asking for "Ricki".'

'Did you ask him about these men?' Lyn queried.

'Oh yes, but Ricardo just laughed. Not a happy laugh, though, and when I asked him where he worked, he would never tell me. Always he was evasive and vague about the location of his office. I was very uneasy, and then after . . . after a visit from two of the men, I . . . I decided to come up here and visit my mama and brother.'

'Why, whatever happened?'

'Oh, it was terrible, Lyn. I was so frightened.' Mercedes' face paled at the memory. 'These two men just kicked our front door open and demanded Ricardo! I told them he was not at home and to please go away, but they wouldn't listen. "You just tell that fine husband of yours that we want either the goods back or our money!" Oh, it was terrible.'

'I'd have been terrified,' Lyn agreed sympathetically. 'What did you do?'

'What could I do? When I said Ricardo was busy in his office they just laughed, and . . . and then they smashed up my lovely sitting room! Mirrors, tables, chairs—everything. When Ricardo came home, he just sat down and said nothing, nothing at all!'

'But didn't he tell you about the money he obviously owed these men?'

'No. He was silent and wouldn't talk to me. I said I would go to Mama and Alvaro for safety and he agreed it was a good idea, but he made me promise not to tell my brother anything. Oh, Lyn, what shall I do?'

Lyn's warm heart was wrung with compassion for poor Mercedes who was sitting slumped in her chair, pale and trembling after having related such a terrifying story.

'I feel very sorry for you, Mercedes, but you really haven't a choice. I can see that you don't want to worry

your mother, but you really must tell Alvaro exactly
what has happened. He'll know what to do.'

'Oh, no . . . no . . . I could not. . . .'

'You must! If only for Ricardo's sake, surely you can
see that. He's obviously got himself into a mess and
needs help. These men sound really bad news, and you
need someone tough to sort them out. You really do.'

'But . . . but you don't understand,' Mercedes wailed.
'Alvaro will never forgive me, never!'

'Of course he will. I'm sure that he's hard and tough
in business, but I know that he'd do anything for a
member of his family. He won't be hard on you,
Mercedes, he'll understand that you love Ricardo,
whatever he's done.'

'*Ah, sí*, you do understand.' Mercedes smiled at Lyn
through her tears. 'You see, Alvaro will make me give
up Ricardo, of that I am certain. But I cannot, Lyn, I
love him too much. I knew you had a kind heart and
would understand such love. . . .'

Lyn hardly heard her words as the older girl
continued to explain how much she loved her husband.
She was totally immersed in her own bewildering
thoughts. What have I been saying? she asked herself
incredulously. How could I possibly tell his sister how
sympathetic and understanding Alvaro will be, especially as he's never treated me with anything but scorn
and anger? And yet . . . and yet she somehow knew that
what she had said was correct. There was another side
to Alvaro which she had instinctively recognised, even
as they had traded such deadly insults at each other.
But how, or why. . . .

'. . . so you see that as much as I love Alvaro, I
cannot tell him about Ricardo. I cannot bear to lose my
husband, I would die first.'

'Oh, Mercedes, please don't cry.' Lyn hurriedly
wheeled her chair over and leant forward, clumsily
putting her arms, one in its plaster cast, about the

sobbing girl. Some moments later, when Mercedes was drying her tears, Lyn rang for Maria and ordered a fresh pot of coffee.

As Mercedes sipped the hot liquid, she gave a sudden exclamation.

'Yes, it is true that I cannot talk to Alvaro myself, but *you* can, Lyn. You can tell him how it is, and save Ricardo and our marriage.'

'*Me* ...?' Lyn spluttered, nearly choking as some of her coffee went the wrong way, down into her windpipe.

'But yes! You are a woman of the world and used to dealing with the big producers of films. *Si?* You will know how to present what has happened to Alvaro so that he will understand.'

'Oh God, no! I couldn't possibly. . . .'

'Please, Lyn,' she begged.

'But ... but you simply don't understand!' Lyn almost wailed with dismay. 'Alvaro ... well, Alvaro and I, we ... er ... we don't always see eye to eye.' She took a deep breath. 'In fact, Mercedes, he ... he doesn't like me at all. I'm *absolutely* the wrong person to talk to him, believe me!'

'But yes, of course he likes you. Very much, my mama says. Indeed, only this morning she said that she thought ...' her voice trailed away as she bent down to pick up her cup of coffee, a slight blush on her cheeks. 'Anyway, I do not believe what you say. You would be able to explain all, very well.'

'Oh, for heaven's sake! You're wrong—I can't begin to tell you just how wrong you are!'

'Oh, please, please help me. . . .' Mercedes' eyes filled with tears again, and as she recalled all her and Doña Elena's kindness, Lyn knew she was powerless to deny the girl's request.

'OK—although I give you fair warning that I am bound to make matters far, far worse. However, I can

see that someone must tell Alvaro, even if the choice of
myself is a rotten one,' she sighed heavily.

'Ah, thank you, thank you.'

'Don't thank me too soon,' Lyn told her grimly. 'And
I may not be able to do it straight away, since I'll have
to wait for the right opportunity. I mean, you don't
want Dolores to know about this, I take it?' she added,
remembering that woman's extraordinary determination
never to let Alvaro and Lyn be alone together. Helpful
though it had been in the past, it might prove to be **very**
awkward when she wanted to talk to him about
Ricardo.

'*Por Dios!* No. Thankfully, Alvaro did not bring her
back with him last night, so we are free of her for a few
days. I do not care what Mama says,' Mercedes added
defiantly, 'I will never believe that my brother could
marry such a woman. She killed her husband, you
know.'

'What . . . murdered him?' Lyn gasped.

'Well, not exactly,' Mercedes grudgingly admitted.
'But she married an old man for his money and then
kept him out dancing in nightclubs until three or four in
the morning. Yes, it is true, she danced him into the
grave! I do not like her at all.'

You're not the only one! Lyn thought grimly. Still,
Alvaro was a big boy now, and in fact, he's the one who
was likely to do the murdering if Dolores ever stepped
out of line! However, her mind was too full of question
marks to give much consideration to Dolores. How on
earth was she to tell Alvaro about the trouble Mercedes
and Ricardo were in? Apart from anything else, getting
him to even agree to listen to her, after their encounter
yesterday, was practically an impossible task.

However, in the event, it proved to be somewhat
easier than she had foreseen.

Some days later the specialist from Monterrey arrived
and decided to remove both her casts, expressing

pleasure at the healing power of her young bones, as he strapped up her ankle and warned her to be careful. 'Take care not to put too much pressure on your ankle—not at once, eh? Use the stick Doña Elena has provided to walk about the house.'

'Can . . . can I ride?'

'Yes, if you are a good horsewoman and not likely to fall off. Why not?'

Lyn had been delighted, and since Alvaro was away on a business trip, she approached Miguel for permission to exercise some of the horses in the stables. He had been doubtful, but once it was obvious she was an excellent rider with light hands, he became full of enthusiasm, choosing for her a mettlesome black mare. For three days she rode at will around the *estancia*, often accompanied by Ramon who had rather tiresomely decided that he was madly in love with his new sister-in-law to be.

Invited one morning to call and see Sanchia at her ranch house down in the valley, Lyn was surprised to find another horse tethered to the hitching post; a large, full-blooded stallion who must, she estimated, stand at least sixteen hands high. She hadn't seen Miguel riding him before, so she concluded that the animal was a new acquisition.

On entering Sanchia's sitting room, she was startled to find not Miguel leaning so casually against the mantelpiece, but the tall figure of Alvaro.

'Good morning, Lyn. I can see that you are on your feet once more, hmm?' he greeted her entrance with a bland, cool smile.

'I . . . er . . . I thought you were away on business . . .' she said huskily. He was dressed in a cream coloured pair of tight jodhpurs which clung to the taut muscles of his thighs, and an open-necked shirt which seemed to be stretched across the wide expanse of his shoulders like a second skin. Her stomach tensed alarmingly, her heart pounding as she vividly recalled just how she had felt when she had last been held by those muscular arms showing beneath the rolled up sleeves of his shirt.

'Ah, I see—when the cat's away, the mice will play, hmm?' he enquired mockingly.

She flushed and caught her breath. He was radiating such a powerful aura of strong, virile masculinity, that she suddenly felt acutely nervous as his eyes flicked over her slight figure. Her ankle was still too swollen to fit into riding boots, and she had been forced to borrow a pair of white plimsolls instead. Wearing these beneath an old skin-tight pair of jeans leant by Mercedes made her feel that not only was she looking a mess, but also far more vulnerable in his presence than usual. She felt his eyes on the thin silk shirt which clung to the high, unconfined peaks of her full breasts, colour flooding her face at having to stand here and have Alvaro assess her with his cool, dismissive stare.

'I . . . I'm sorry, Sanchia. I seemed to have called at an inappropriate time.' Ignoring Alvaro, she turned to smile at Miguel's shy wife. 'I'll come back later.'

'Oh no, Lyn. You are most welcome. . . .'

'Some other time, maybe.' Lyn smiled brightly at her again, and left the room, hurrying out of the house to unhitch her horse. Anything to escape Alvaro's hateful presence, she told herself, her breathing ragged as she tried frantically to untangle the mare's reins.

Moments later, a large hand grasped her nervous fingers as Alvaro calmly moved her aside and deftly performed the task.

'Where are you intending to ride?' he asked, in the same calm, bland voice with which he had greeted her earlier.

'Oh . . . er . . . nowhere special,' she murmured, wishing with all her heart that he would ride away and leave her in peace.

'Ah, in that case, I will join you. Give me your leg.'

'There's no need. I am quite capable of. . . .' But she spoke too late as his powerful arms lifted her up like thistledown, and placed her astride her saddle almost before she knew what was happening.

'Well, really! Let me tell you. . . .'

'No, I will tell you something,' he said firmly. 'I have too few days like this, when I can be free from business. Therefore, I have decided that we will have a truce, yes? Today, we will ride, enjoy the scenery and the clear mountain air, and have no angry words or conflict, hmm?'

'Well, I. . . .' She glanced through her eyelashes at his face which was creased into a broad smile. A smile that seemed to hit her like a blow, leaving her dazed and confused.

'Of course,' he added, 'tomorrow will undoubtedly be different. I may well be in a black rage and threatening to beat you. So enjoy today, little one, hmm?' He laughed, his grin so infectious that she found herself smiling back.

'OK, a truce it is,' she agreed.

They cantered down over the lush grass of the valley before halting for a rest, and then letting the horses saunter along slowly as Alvaro pointed out the surrounding mountains of the Sierra Madre.

'That one over there is *Cerro de la Silla.*' He indicated a saddle-shaped crest. 'According to legend it was formed by a local man, a miser, who was so unfortunate as to lose a peso on the topmost ridge. He was so upset that he dug and dug, ever more frantically, until he found his one peso again!'

'A likely story!' she laughed, following his horse as he turned sharply left and led the way down over a rocky slope. It took all her skill to control the sliding hooves of her mare, and it wasn't until Alvaro halted that she looked up, gasping with delight.

Over the side of a cliff high above them tumbled

down a stream of water ending in a small pool, before it fell again into another pool and yet again for a third time into the bubbling foam by their horses feet.

'It's a triple waterfall!' she marvelled. 'I've never seen anything so lovely, and the setting. . . .' Words failed her as she stared about her. The waterfall was surrounded on three sides by lush, verdant greenery. Long vines hung down from the brilliant vegetation, making it all look, she thought, like some garden of Eden.

'I used to come here much as a child,' he said slowly. 'It is a special place, is it not?'

'Oh yes,' she breathed. 'It's perfect.'

'Come, we will dismount and drink some of the clear water.' He slid out of his saddle, and she dismounted equally swiftly, so that there was no need for him to assist her. The thought of his hands on her body causing her a momentary feeling of deep inner panic.

If Alvaro had noticed her reaction he gave no sign as he led her towards the pool. She was surprised to see him reach up towards a crack in the rock above his head; the mystery being solved as he removed a tin mug, which he bent to fill from the water at his feet.

Later, as they sat on a smooth rock, taking turns at drinking the ice cold water, Lyn realised that she would never have a better opportunity to tell him about the problems of Ricardo and Mercedes. Watching him take out his slim cigar case and light a cheroot, she took a deep breath and turned towards him.

'Er . . . Alvaro. . . .' she began, before her courage seemed to ebb away.

'Hmm?'

She swallowed nervously. 'Can I . . . can I talk to you for a minute?'

'But my dear girl, you already are!'

'No, I . . . er . . . I meant that I wanted to talk seriously,' she replied huskily, suddenly disconcerted by an unexpected gleam in his dark eyes as he gazed intently at her face.

He drew deeply on his cigar, exhaling the smoke with a heavy sigh. 'Ah, well, if you must. Felipe, as you know, is still in Spain, and. . . .'

'Oh, for heaven's sake! Can't you think of anything else but your precious brother?' she snapped nervously.

'Not very lover-like, my dear Lyn! However, it is natural that I should suppose you wished to discuss your fiancé, and the situation, hmm?'

'There is no "situation" as you call it. I intend to leave just as soon as I can, even climbing down the mountain if I have to!' she ground out, before realising that arguing with Alvaro would not further Mercedes' cause. She took a deep breath. 'No, what I want to talk about does not concern me, well, not directly that is.' She paused, trying to marshal her thoughts.

'Very well, we will leave the aggravating question of you and my brother for another time. What is it you wish to talk about, little one?'

I wish to heaven he wouldn't keep calling me 'little one', she thought distractedly. His soft words and accent seemed to be affecting her in a quite alarming manner.

Screwing up her courage, and staring out at the swirling pool of water, she slowly began to relate the troublesome story as outlined by Mercedes. There was a long silence when she had finished and she turned to see him staring blindly down at the rock on which he was sitting.

'Please . . . please don't be angry with me for telling you all this. I did try and persuade Mercedes to tell you herself, I really did. But she was certain that because you didn't approve of Ricardo in the first place, you would try to take her away from him; to somehow break up her marriage. And although I personally think that Ricardo's a nasty piece of work, she really does love him.'

The silence seemed to lengthen, and Lyn could feel her body trembling as she waited for his outburst at her meddling, which she was sure would erupt at any minute. When he did speak, he took her completely by surprise.

'How tragic that Mercedes could ever think that I would hurt her,' he murmured. 'And how very kind of you, my dear Lyn, to have sought to help the family in this way.'

She glanced quickly at him, startled not only by the absence of his usual sardonic tone, but also by the gleam in his dark eyes. A gleam that made her heart leap and her blood race in her veins.

'Yes, I have had some odd reports about Ricardo,' he continued in a hard voice. 'It is obvious that once I have cleared up this present trouble, I must remove him from his undesirable acquaintances in Mexico City, and give him a job where he is very firmly under my eye.'

'Mercedes will be so grateful,' she assured him.

'Hmm. Do you know, I find it interesting that despite the considerable ... er ... disagreements which have taken place between us, that you should have advised her, quite correctly of course, to tell me about her troubles.'

'Well, it was ... it was the obvious answer, wasn't it?' she countered swiftly.

'Very true, and yet, I ask myself, how could you be so certain that I would be understanding? How is it that you should appear to know me almost better than I know myself, hmm? I find your behaviour in this case odd. It is as if you were acting out of character, somehow.'

'Oh great!' She jumped to her feet, feeling suddenly deeply hurt and angry. 'I told Mercedes that my talking to you would only cause me trouble! Is it so *very* extraordinary that I should be capable of human sympathy, just like everyone else? Why shouldn't I have a warm heart like any normal woman?' She turned away to hide the weak tears of self pity which filled her eyes. Although why she should shed even one tear because of this damn man, she had absolutely no idea!

A moment later she felt her shoulders grasped as he turned her swiftly towards his tall, dominant figure.

'*Una lágrima?*' he queried softly as a large tear escaped and ran down her cheek. 'A tear from this warm-hearted woman?'

'Please . . . no, Alvaro . . .' she whispered huskily as a hand lightly tilted her face upwards, his other arm gently closing about her trembling figure. She should run, she should push him away or twist out of his arm, she told herself desperately. But she did none of these things. Staring up into the gleaming ebony of his dark eyes, mesmerised by what she saw there, she let him slowly pull her closer.

'Please . . . yes, Lyn . . .' he breathed thickly, slowly lowering his black head. She quivered, her eyes gazing at the firm line of his mouth, nervously aware that it was moving inexorably down towards her own. When at last his warm lips touched hers, she gave a barely audible sigh, which seemed to unlock a hidden door as a wild rush of excitement flooded through her veins. Slowly, almost involuntarily, she arched herself against him, giving herself to the demanding possession of his kiss without restraint, her body trembling as his hands moved slowly and sensually as they caressed her soft curves. The anger and hostility which had lain so long between them seemed to be fusing into a very different element, a chemistry that refused to be denied.

His kiss deepened, his arms closing about her slight figure like bands of steel, crushing her breasts against his hard chest and moulding her thighs against his, making her shockingly aware of his own arousal. His lips burned and demanded—what? as a deep groan broke from his throat.

Suddenly frightened of the strange forces which seemed to have been unleashed between them, she jerked her head away, her neck drooping backwards as he still held her so firmly, her hair a bright shining stream down her back. He lowered his head and delicately ran his lips down over her arched throat, while she moaned helplessly as a deep, aching need gripped her, clamouring for release.

Slowly, he straightened and stood looking down into her dazed face, at her wide blue eyes glowing with languorous desire, the soft trembling of her lips. It seemed to be an enormous effort for her to focus properly on Alvaro's face, pale beneath his tan and blank of all expression as his heavily lidded eyes searched her face intently.

Lyn felt herself grow hot as a crimson tide of shame and embarrassment swept through her body, now shivering with nervous tension. She was totally at a loss for words—indeed what could she possibly say, even if she had been capable of speech?

Alvaro seemed equally silent as without any change in his tightly closed face, he carefully lifted her shaking figure on to her horse, before mounting his own animal and, still not having said a word, led the way back up over the rocks to the green valley above.

Riding home in silence, Lyn was absorbed by her own chaotic thoughts, looking up with relief as she saw they were approaching the stables of the *hacienda*. A firm hand suddenly seized her rein, bringing her to a halt.

'I apologise, señorita,' Alvaro rasped, his hoarse voice devoid of all expression as he stared fixedly ahead at the space between his horse's ears. 'What happened by the waterfall was . . . was most regrettable, and must never happen again.'

Lyn couldn't reply, a thick lump seemed to be obstructing her throat and she felt very close to tears as he suddenly spun his horse around, and with a sharp dig of his heels sent the stallion flying back down the valley, shadowed by the mountains beyond.

CHAPTER SIX

COLLECTING her walking stick from the tack room, Lyn left the vast stable block and moved slowly across the courtyard towards the house. Limping slightly, her legs feeling as though they carried heavy lead weights, she wandered through the huge echoing, empty rooms like a sleepwalker. Her whole body throbbed with tension, a deep physical weariness that she had never known before. Even after a day spent galloping horses for film take after take, such as she had done last year for John Hardy who was a notoriously difficult film director, she had been able to seek relief in a sound night's sleep, waking refreshed the next morning. But such a simple remedy wasn't applicable to her present trembling exhaustion. Alvaro's experienced lovemaking had aroused her senses to such a fever pitch of nervous excitement that every nerve end in her body seemed to be screaming out for satisfaction and fulfilment. Reaching, at last, the sanctuary of her bedroom, she staggered across the floor to collapse in a heap on her bed.

She must pull herself together! It was just a simple matter of sexual attraction, that's all, she told herself desperately. Goodness knows she had seen many of her friends held firmly within such toils as they had hungered after the most unsuitable men. Up to now she had remained unscathed by such storms of passion, and had even been faintly contemptuous of those who had succumbed; not realising what a devastating effect such a strong physical urge could create.

Well, she knew now, didn't she? Lyn groaned with embarrassed shame as she recalled how she had yielded in Alvaro's arms, hating herself and her body for its purely sexual response to his raw masculinity. Until she had come to the *hacienda*, her vision of the relationship between a man and a woman had been couched in terms of holding hands, bouquets of flowers and soft kisses in the moonlight, all leading to an altar where dressed in white lace she would plight her troth to the man of her dreams.

It had all been far too ridiculously romantic, of course, and probably the fault of her upbringing by the dour great-aunts in that grim old Rectory facing out over the Yorkshire moors, back in England. It was only when Uncle Charley had suddenly appeared that she had realised there was more to life than being at the beck and call of two difficult old women.

She could remember neither of her parents, who had been killed in a road accident when she was only three. Passed around various members of her family, she had ended up, at the age of seven with the great-aunts in Yorkshire. Lyn still shivered when she remembered the long dark passages, the cold rooms full of unfashionably heavy, dark furniture that smelled of cats; the only creatures that the aunts had any affection for.

Luckily, a trust fund had paid for her boarding school education, where she was able to escape to the warm, friendly atmosphere of a normal childhood; but always she had to return to the chilly, dampening greyness that was her only home. Leaving school with few academic achievements, she had been trapped as an octopus claims its victim, sucked back and down into the depths of dark monotony, the unending, unvarying routine as she fetched and carried, swept and polished.

Maybe, given time, she would have found the resolution to run away. However, Uncle Charley's arrival, visiting the old family home after many years in America, had dramatically changed her existence. It was as if he had waved a magic wand, when he had offered her a home with him in California. 'This place is like Wuthering Heights—only nastier!' he had declared forthrightly. 'It sure ain't a place for a pretty young girl,' he added, sweeping all the aunts' objections aside. Almost before she realised what was happening she found herself transported to perpetual sunshine where, at the age of seventeen, she had fallen madly in love for the first and only time—with horses.

I should have stuck to them, she told herself miserably. The four-legged animals were a lot safer than getting involved with Alvaro. . . .

Her thoughts were interrupted by a sudden knock which echoed her pounding heart beats as Mercedes put her head around the door.

'Ah, Lyn, are you not joining us for a meal?'

'I . . . er . . . I think I rather . . . er . . . overdid it, out riding this morning. Would you and your mother mind if I missed lunch today?'

'No, of course not,' Mercedes assured her and turned to go.

'Oh, by the way, I . . . er . . . I managed to talk to Alvaro, and he's going to take care of everything. So you and Ricardo won't have to worry any more.'

'*Really* . . .?' Mercedes gasped. 'He was not too cross . . .?'

Lyn managed to sketch a reassuring smile. 'No, I told you he would be very understanding. In fact, I think that he was upset that you hadn't told him yourself.'

'. . . and he won't part me from my Ricardo?'

'Of course not! How could he break up your marriage if you didn't want him to?' Lyn looked at the girl whose face shone with happiness. 'Why don't you tell your mother all about it, now that you know everything will be all right? After all, she must suspect, as I did, that you've been worried about something. And then, maybe, you can have a long talk with Alvaro.'

'Ah, Lyn—what a kind girl you are!' Mercedes gave her a warm hug. 'How can I ever thank you?'

'It's a very small thing I did. You and your mother have done far more for me,' she said firmly. 'Now, I'm going to have a hot bath to ease my aching muscles. After being in plaster for so long, I've decided that to be able to have a bath is one of the great luxuries of life!'

The husky catch in her forced laugh sounded odd even to her ears, and she could only hope that Mercedes was so preoccupied with her own concerns that she hadn't noticed.

The bathroom was a luxurious palace, compared to those she had known before. She ran the bath, poured in some rose-scented bath oil and then slipped out of her clothes and into the warm water with a sigh of relief.

This palatial bathroom in Mexico was a far cry from the freezing cold room with its white, heavy Victorian tub set up on claw feet, and the geyser which had rumbled and wheezed in the corner of the bathroom in Yorkshire. She'd certainly come a long way in the last four years, Lyn thought, lying back and revelling in the fragrant clouds of steam which rose from the water.

Her new life in California had been a revelation. Although shy and introverted to start with, she had bloomed under the benign kindness of her uncle as she learnt to ride and became totally absorbed in the life of his ranch. A sort of late adolescence, she supposed, as Uncle Charley, proving in his own way to be just as strict as her great aunts, had kept her well away from the circus. This he ran mostly for fun, since his main income came from the breeding of horses. It was only when two of his bareback riders suddenly left for more pay with a circus in Germany that her uncle had finally given in to her pleading and allowed her to join the nomadic life.

Surprisingly, as if recognising her innocence, the girls

in the troupe while teasing her for her lack of worldly knowledge, had been very kind hearted. When she proved her overwhelming skill with horses—an astonishing gift her uncle called it—they had affectionately protected and guarded her against the rougher elements to be found in circus life. Even the last two years she had spent as a stunt girl had meant that she worked so hard that she had little time for relaxation. Of course she'd had plenty of dates, but none of the men she met had caused the slightest dent in her heart, and watching her friends in the throes of love affairs—most of them unhappy ones—she had not been eager to experiment for herself.

It was no wonder that the advent in her life of someone like Alvaro had knocked her sideways, she consoled herself. He was no callow youth or polite young man to desist from unwanted attentions after one freezing glance from her blue eyes. He was a virile, experienced man of thirty-five who was quite capable of seeing what he wanted—and taking it!

Her face flushed as she tried to prevent her mind recalling his tall, powerful figure in the tight riding trousers and close fitting open-necked shirt. She must be mad! The fact that she was now lying here, racked by a deep longing for his hard embrace, quivering and shaking from the effect of his inflaming kisses, was hardly his fault. With as much self-honesty as she could muster, she told herself that their encounter by the waterfall would have meant less than nothing to him, not when he had Dolores to satisfy his physical needs!

It had just been a matter of time and place, no more than that. He had seen her in tears, and felt sorry for her. How could it be anything else? How could he have possibly guessed that a woman he believed to be a film star, with all the sophistication that implied, should in fact be a girl who was so green and inexperienced that she had been totally devastated by the emotions he had aroused? She was suddenly overwhelmed by an urgent, desperate longing that he should realise that it was she, Lyn, whom he had kissed, and not his brother's fiancée, Marilyn Thorne.

Getting out of the bath, she towelled herself briskly dry, asking herself for the hundredth time what mad folly could have possibly persuaded her to agree to this substitution for Marilyn, this crazy masquerade? If she had learnt anything today, it was that she must leave this place, and Mexico, as soon as possible.

By the time she left the bath and returned to her bedroom in her dressing-gown she had come to some firm conclusions. She may have been trapped here while she was in plaster, but now she was free of that restriction, she must try to escape just as soon as she could. Time was the pressing problem. She tried to count the days since she had left the hospital. She couldn't remember exactly just when Marilyn had said that she would be returning there, but it must be soon. What on earth would she and Larry Wilde do when they found she had gone?

Discarding various impractical ideas as she climbed back on her bed to rest, she decided that her only option was to telephone her uncle's ranch. One of the nurses looking after Uncle Charley would be able to pass on her messages, and the best time to phone was later on this afternoon, when everyone would be having their siesta.

It was early evening when she woke, and she lay for some moments watching the shadows in her room lengthen before she recalled what she had planned to do. Pray heaven that she hadn't left it too late!

Lyn dressed quickly, hardly noticing what she was wearing as she slipped into a thin cotton dress and hurried out of her room and along the corridor, her heart hammering against her ribs. On reaching Alvaro's study, she knocked gently and, receiving no reply, cautiously eased the door open. Moving silently across the large room, she was bewildered by the fact that there were three telephones on the ornate desk. Did they all have outside lines? Regarding them with a worried frown for a moment, she took the plunge. Lifting the receiver nearest to her, she sighed with relief as she heard the international dialling tone. Pressing the digits to summon the operator, and then speaking as softly as she could, she gave the necessary code and number.

'Un momento,' she heard before she nearly jumped out of her skin with fright, her eyes gazing mesmerised at the large, powerful hand which had come down on the instrument, cutting off her call.

'Just exactly what do you think you are doing?' Alvaro enquired softly.

'Trying to telephone—as if it wasn't perfectly obvious!' she snapped nervously, still feeling shaken by his sudden appearance. 'And anyway, how did you get in here without my hearing you?'

'But my dear Lyn, I was already in the room.' He indicated a high-backed, swivel chair by the window. 'The fact that I did not answer your knock meant that I did not wish to be disturbed,' he remarked coldly. 'And now, I suggest that you return to your room.'

'Why in the hell should I?' she retorted, disturbed by his proximity and the weakening effect it was having on her legs which suddenly felt as if they were made of cotton wool.

'Because I say so.'

'And that's that, I suppose?' she lashed back angrily. 'Well, let me tell you that I'm not a prisoner, and you can't. . . .'

'But yes, you are indeed a prisoner, and I can keep you here just as long as I wish to. How can you be so foolish as to think otherwise?' he said, the menace in his soft, silky tone of voice making the hairs prickle at the back of her neck.

Get 4 free books...
a free tote bag...

SEE INSIDE FOR THE
SECRET OF THIS
HARLEQUIN HEART.

plus a special Mystery Gift when you give your heart to Harlequin.

Here's a sweetheart of an offer!

Take these 4 FREE ROMANCE NOVELS, plus a FREE TOTE BAG, with no obligation to buy!

Say Hello to Yesterday

Holly Weston had raised her small son and worked her way to features writer for a major newspaper.

She had been very young when she married Nick Falconer but old enough to lose her heart completely when he left. Despite her success in her new life, her old one haunted her.

But it was over and done with—until an assignment in Greece brought her face to face with Nick, and all she was trying to forget...

Man's World

Kate's new boss, editor Eliot Holman, might have devastating charms—but Kate couldn't care less, even if he was interested in her.

Everyone, including Eliot, thought Kate was grieving over the loss of her husband, Toby. She kept it a secret just how cruelly Toby had treated her and how terrified she was of trusting men again.

But Eliot refused to leave her alone. He was no different from other men... or was he?

Born Out of Love

Charlotte stared at the man through a mist of confusion was Logan. An older Logan, of course, but unmistakably man who had ravaged her emotions and then abandoned her all those years ago.

She ought to feel angry. She ought to feel resentful and cheated. Instead, she was apprehensive—terrified at the complications he could create...

Time of the Temptress

Rebellion against a cushioned, controlled life had landed Eve Tarrant in Africa. Now only the tough mercenary Wade O'Mara stood between her and possible death in the wild, revolution-torn jungle.

But the real danger was Wade himself—he had made Eve aware of herself as a woman...

Your Four Free Harlequin Novels will take you into a world of romance, love and desire. If you choose to become a Harlequin Home Subscriber, you'll be able to indulge in romantic adventure again and again with new novels every month. Experience the world of Harlequin by returning the reply card below. You'll receive your 4 FREE BOOKS, FREE TOTE and MYSTERY GIFT. Mail your card today!

Take these 4 books and tote bag FREE!

Affix the special heart here and we'll also send you a special Mystery Gift!

Mail to Harlequin Reader Service
2504 W. Southern Ave., Tempe, AZ 85282

Yes, please send me FREE and without obligation my 4 Harlequin Presents novels. If you do not hear from me, please send me 6 new Harlequin Presents novels each month as soon as they come off the presses. I understand that I will be billed only $10.50 for all 6 books. There are no shipping and handling nor any other hidden charges. There is no minimum number of books that I have to purchase. In fact, I can cancel this arrangement at any time. The 4 books, tote bag, and mystery gift are mine to keep as FREE gifts, even if I do not buy any additional books.

106 CIP BA5M

Name	(please print)	
Address		Apt. No.
City	State	Zip

Signature (if under 18, parent or guardian must sign)

Affix special Heart on reply card to receive your Mystery Gift!

BUSINESS REPLY CARD

FIRST CLASS   PERMIT NO. 70   TEMPE, AZ

POSTAGE WILL BE PAID BY ADDRESSEE

Harlequin Reader Service
2504 West Southern Avenue
Tempe, AZ 85282

NO POSTAGE
NECESSARY
IF MAILED
IN THE
UNITED STATES

'But ... but you can't ...' she repeated weakly, gazing up into Alvaro's stern face. It was as though their earlier intimacy had never existed and they were complete strangers. The coldness in his dark eyes was like a knife in her heart as he firmly grasped her arm, leading her back towards the door.

'You ... you can't prevent me from getting to a telephone eventually. Even you can't stay awake all day and all night!' she taunted wildly, trying to twist out of the hand whose fingers were biting so cruelly into her soft flesh.

He paused, looking down at her for a long moment. 'What you say is, of course, quite correct. Very well, I see that I will have to instruct my servants that they must form a rota, so that there is always someone guarding all the telephones in this house. Is that what you want? Will the use of my servants in such a way please you?' Grabbing her other arm, he shook her in a sudden spasm of rage.

'Alvaro ... I ...' she faltered, running her tongue over lips that were suddenly dry.

'Unless you give me your promise, your word of honour not to touch the telephones, that is exactly what I shall do!'

Looking up into his unrelenting hard features, his eyes as cold as ice, she knew that she was beaten. How could she allow the men and women who had always greeted her in such a friendly manner, to be imposed on in such a way? She couldn't allow them to be treated as such by this ... this tyrant.

Lyn sighed wearily, her shoulders drooping in defeat. 'Yes, all right, you win. I ... I'll give you my ... my promise,' she muttered.

'*Bien, gracias.* I am sorry, *querida*,' he murmured quietly as he let go of her arms.

Confused by the unexpected warmth in his voice and exhausted by the emotional, turbulent events of the day, she stumbled wearily against his hard figure. For a moment it seemed as if she couldn't move, paralysed by the fresh tang of his cologne and the feel of his warm skin through his thin silk shirt.

'*Por Dios!*' Alvaro swore savagely, gazing down into the wide blue eyes clouding with desire and the innocent provocation of her soft, trembling lips. '*Out!* Get out of here at once!' he thundered, pushing her roughly through into the hall and slamming the door in her face.

Lyn stood gazing blankly at the closed mahogany door for some time, before tears blinded her eyes and she turned to limp slowly away.

Lyn gave her horse its head as she galloped over the green turf of the valley. The warm breeze in her face, the fresh green smell of the grass and the warmth of the mare's smooth body beneath hers, brought relief and succour to her turbulent emotions.

Wishing to avoid Alvaro like the plague, Lyn had kept firmly to her room yesterday, only receiving a visit from Doña Elena while she was having breakfast this morning. She had been almost embarrassingly grateful for Lyn's assistance in solving her daughter's problems. However, she had not troubled to hide her disquiet about Mercedes' future life with Ricardo. 'He is weak and greedy,' she said with a sad shake of her head. 'He will always be a problem, I'm afraid.'

Among her general conversation Doña Elena had let fall the information that Alvaro had flown down to Monterrey the previous evening. He was, apparently, dealing with Ricardo's trouble, and wasn't expected back until much later in the day.

Slowly munching her toast after the older woman had gone, Lyn thought that she now had the perfect opportunity to explore the *estancia*. She may have had to promise Alvaro that she wouldn't attempt to use the telephones, but that didn't mean she had given up her

intention to escape. Far from it. Their confrontation in
his study had only stiffened her resolve to leave as soon
as possible. She resolutely refused to examine her
complicated feelings for the man who had so dominated
her life for the last five weeks, firmly concentrating on
her plans instead. Somewhere, there must be a route
down the mountains to Monterrey—and if at all
possible, she intended to find it.

Feeling slightly more optimistic at the thought of
some positive action, she went out to the stables only to
find that Alvaro had guessed her intentions. He had
ordered the door of the tack room to be locked.
Containing as it did all the saddles and bridles, he
obviously must have thought that he had checkmated
any move she might make to try and leave without his
permission.

'Tough luck, Alvaro!' Lyn said out loud with a grim
smile as she led the mare out of her stall, slipping a rope
halter she had found over the head of the animal. There
was no way he could possibly have known that she was
far more used to riding bareback than on one of the
high-pommelled saddles used here in Mexico.

She was still feeling a perverse satisfaction at having
managed to out-wit Alvaro as she brought the galloping
horse down to a quieter canter, and then an ambling
walk. She was almost sure, after snatching a brief look
at an old-fashioned map hanging up in the hall of the
house, that somewhere between the helicopter pad and
the corrals containing the fighting bulls bred on the
estancia, there must be a track wide enough for a car.
Food was brought up to the valley by truck, and where
a vehicle went, so could she.

'*Hola!*'

'Oh no!' Lyn muttered under her breath as she saw
Ramon cantering towards her. His presence was likely
to destroy all her carefully laid plans.

'Ah, Lyn, how nice to see you.' He looked at her

figure mounted on the mare with no saddle or bridle, except the rope halter. His eyebrows arched in surprise. 'I thought that . . .' his voice died away.

'You thought that Alvaro had managed to keep me firmly in the house,' she said dryly.

'Yes,' he shrugged. 'He is worried about your ankle.'

'Oh, is that what he says?' She snorted with derision. Opening her mouth to tell Ramon exactly what she thought about his brother, she hastily closed it again. She wanted to find the way out of this place, didn't she? How better than in the company of Ramon, who obviously admired her so much, and whose brother had apparently not told him the real reason why her freedom was being curtailed? She'd have to be careful, of course. If she asked too many questions, Ramon might get suspicious.

'Why don't we ride together?' she said, giving him a warm smile and trying not to feel too guilty at using his fondness for her in this way.

'Con mucho gusto!' he replied with a happy laugh. 'Where shall we go?'

'Well,' she paused as she pretended to consider the question. 'I'd love to see the bulls you breed for the bullfights. Could we go that way, and then you can tell me all about it.'

'Sí, can you manage your horse, riding like that?' he asked with concern.

'Oh yes, I . . . er . . . I think so,' she murmured, trying to hide a smile. After almost two years with the circus, there wasn't much she couldn't do on a horse. When her uncle had decided to retire and disband the circus, Lyn had been heartbroken. The question of what on earth she was to do with herself had been her main preoccupation that summer. She couldn't imagine how she could face a job in an office, not now she had got used to a steady diet of dangerous thrills and spills. 'You ain't nothing but a tom-boy,' her uncle had said.

'Time you grew up and settled down with a nice man,' he had added with concern. But she had merely laughed, delighted when she was contacted by an agent who had taken his children to see the Wild West Show being performed by the circus.

'If you can ride like that, honey, I've got enough business to put your way that will keep you working flat out!' he'd said. True to his word, she had found herself appearing in countless films, mostly westerns, but more often lately, as her name had become known among the studios, she had been engaged to perform daring stunts for female stars who were too valuable a property to risk being hurt.

'Tell me about the bulls you breed,' she asked Ramon trying, but not quite succeeding, to hide the fact that she hated the whole idea of bullfights.

'Ah, you are like many *norteamericanos*. You do not understand that it is part of our culture, here in Mexico. Almost every little Mexican boy, if he doesn't want to be a famous footballer, he wishes to grow up to be a matador!'

'Well, I've got to be honest and admit that I've never seen a bullfight. I just always felt ... well, I've always felt so sorry for the bulls, somehow.'

'Do not feel too sorry!' he laughed wryly. 'The *toros bravos*, the fighting bulls are a special breed, you understand. They are nothing like the ordinary domestic bull you will have seen in the fields with cows—no, not at all! For many, many generations they have been bred for battle, and they fight because it is their nature, their will to do so, not because they are frightened in the ring. Come, you will see.'

They rode over to a corral of about six acres, bounded on all sides by a sturdy wooden fence approximately four feet high. They dismounted and went over to lean on the fence, looking at the animals grazing nearby.

'These young bulls are two years old,' Ramon explained, pointing to what seemed a collection of huge, mammoth-like animals. 'These have just been selected for *la corrida*, although they will not fight until they are older. The animals you see here are the ones who have proved that they will charge immediately. They do not need to be annoyed or prodded into action. Very, very dangerous,' he added seriously.

They chatted for some time. Lyn was just beginning to lead up to a question as to exactly where the route out of the valley was, when she heard a buzzing in her ears. Raising her head, she saw a flash of red rising up over the nearest mountain peak. Alvaro's red helicopter passed slowly overhead towards its landing pad and Lyn realised she was running out of time and into trouble! There was no way Alvaro could have missed seeing her, and she quickly gathered up the rope halter, vaulting on to her horse as she prepared to ride away down the valley to escape his wrath. She had no doubts at all that he would be furious that she had outwitted him.

Turning to call goodbye to Ramon, she gasped with horror. On the far side of the corral containing the bulls, was a small child whose presence had been concealed by a rise in the ground. Now she was up on her horse, Lyn could see that while the child was staring up fascinated by the helicopter, a bull from the other side of the field was trotting purposefully towards the child; a little girl with flowers in her hands.

Giving herself no time to think of the consequences, and guided solely by instinct, Lyn reined in her horse and digging her heels viciously into the mare's sides, rode straight for the fence.

She hardly heard Ramon's startled shout as she rode past him. Easily clearing the wooden fence, Lyn forced the mare into a hard gallop as she made directly for the child ignoring the startled, raised heads of the grazing bulls.

The ground seemed to fly past beneath the horse's pounding hooves, and she prayed with every ounce of her being that she would be in time to save the child. She knew what she had to do. She had seen a visiting Cossack troupe perform it, and had given them no rest until they had taught her the technique. She had subsequently performed it scores of times in the circus and for the camera. Pray God her skill wouldn't desert her now.

With a few yards to go, she heard the awesome bellowing and thudding feet of the bull as it neared its prey. She must shut her mind to the sound—she must concentrate on the all-important timing since she would only have one chance.

The child was standing still, staring with fascinated horror, like a rabbit in the headlights of a car as the bull charged towards her. 'Don't move, don't move!' Lyn cried, although she knew the little girl couldn't hear her, and then there was no more time for either thought or prayer. Checking the horse slightly, she leapt nimbly off, took one bouncing step as she bent down to scoop up the little girl, and leapt back on to the horse, the child firmly held in the crook of her arm.

The bull was just a brown blur as it thundered past, unable to stop its charge in time. Wheeling her horse about, Lyn galloped towards the nearest fence as if the hounds of hell were after her, the child a mute, shivering bundle in her arms. Lyn knew the horse was tiring, but she willed it on, holding her breath as the fence approached. She needn't have worried, as they cleared it with inches to spare and she brought them to a shuddering halt.

It wasn't until she slid off the sweating animal, the little girl still firmly clasped in her arms, that Lyn returned to normality and she realised what she had done. Her hands were shaking as if she was in the grip of a raging fever as she set the whimpering child down on the ground, before forcing her wobbly legs to lead her horse over to a nearby haystack. Grabbing a handful of the hay, she began to rub down the animal's hot, steaming coat as Ramon galloped up.

'*Dios, Dios!*' Ramon's pale face was a mixture of admiration and fright. 'My heart was in my mouth, *querida. . . .*'

His words were interrupted by the arrival of a landrover. It screeched to a standstill with a squeal of brakes and Alvaro leapt out of the vehicle, striding swiftly towards them.

'Wasn't she magnificent?' Ramon cried. '*Vaya mujer!* What a woman!'

Alvaro came to a halt, his face as white as a sheet as he stared fixedly at Lyn and the little girl. 'Take the child back in the landrover down to the *pueblo*,' he rasped at Ramon. 'I will ride your horse back to the *hacienda*.'

'But, Alvaro, your clothes?' His brother gazed at Alvaro's formal, lightweight suit over a crisp white shirt and slim silk tie; at his feet lightly shod in immaculate Gucci loafers.

'*Por Dios! Me vale verga!* I don't give a damn! Certainly not about my clothes!' Alvaro snapped impatiently, bending down and gently picking up the little girl. Murmuring soothing sounds, he carried her over to the vehicle, watching as Ramon climbed in and started the engine. It was only when the landrover was moving out of sight that he spun on his heels to look at Lyn.

'I . . . I hope that child will be all right . . .' she gasped, leaning against the side of her horse, her breasts heaving with exhaustion.

'What in the name of God do you think you were doing? You could have been killed. Don't you understand that, *you stupid girl?*' he shouted, striding forward to grasp her shoulders as he shook her in a violent fury.

'What ...?' she panted breathlessly, completely stunned as she looked up at his white face, the lines of strain deeply etched about his mouth.

'How dare you disobey my orders? How dare you ride my horse without my express permission?' he roared, firmly in the grip of a terrifying loss of temper.

'Would you rather the child had been killed?' she screamed back as the heat of his anger scorched her own raw nerves. 'What was I supposed to do? Just stand there and let the bull gore the child, or maybe you would think it more fun if she was just trampled to death?'

'You disobeyed my orders!' he repeated furiously. 'And where did you learn to ride like that! *Cristos!*'

'Don't you shout or swear at me, you ... you bloody man!' she lashed back, almost fainting with pain at the cruel bite of his fingers. 'Can't you ever think of anything but your damn pride? Who cares whether I had your *permission*, for God's sake! OK,' she gave a high, scornful laugh. 'Next time I see a little girl about to be killed by a bull, I'll send you forms in triplicate asking if I can do something about it. Of course, the bull isn't going to ask for your permission—but that's just too bad, I suppose! And get your filthy hands off me—*pronto!*'

When he just stood staring down at her, she raised her hands and brought them down with a short chopping motion on his arms. With a gasp of pain and swearing violently under his breath, he let her go.

'Yes, I'm full of surprises,' she snarled coldly as his dark, angry eyes widened with shock. 'Not only can I ride, but I can also perform karate. So, you just watch yourself, sweetie, or I'll chop you in half!' she added through clenched teeth which chattered with tension. She was totally in the possession of an overwhelming urge to hurt and wound him, every bit as much as his extraordinary reaction to the danger she had been in was hurting her. God knows, she hadn't expected effusive thanks, but neither did she deserve the anger and fury he was pouring over her head. No way!

'*Por Dios*, Lyn ...' he ground out in furious exasperation.

Possessed by some evil demon, she glared at him, trembling with anger as she prepared to verbally knife him as hard as she could. He needed to be taught a lesson, by God, he did!

'You thought that I was a real patsy, didn't you, Alvaro? Completely at your mercy when I was wearing plaster casts, so you could march around doing your *macho* bit. Well, it may have impressed that black widow spider, Dolores, but let me tell you that it just gave me a good laugh!'

'*Basta!* That is enough!'

'Hah!' She laughed in his face. 'It's no good trying to shout or threaten me any more, because now that I can defend myself, I've decided to change the rules—*smart ass!* So, why don't you get on your horse and ride home to mummy like a good little boy? In fact. . . .'

She never completed the sentence. With a bellow of rage, Alvaro charged towards her like one of the fighting bulls in the corral. Swiftly deciding that her only safety lay in flight, she whirled and ran as fast as she could towards her horse grazing quietly by the haystack. She was impeded by a jabbing pain from her weak ankle which slowed her up, and his swift reactions. One moment she heard his rough breathing behind her, the next he had seized her arm, spinning her body through the air before she fell winded on to a pile of loose hay.

Panting, she lay on her back, deeply flushed and gasping as she fought to catch her breath. The next instant, Alvaro threw himself on top of her, with an angry growl, pinning her to the ground and tethering her arms above her head with his hands.

After a brief, furtive glance at his angry tanned face looming over hers, Lyn closed her eyes in weary despair as she struggled to catch her breath.

Alvaro had no such problems. 'I told you the first day in our house that you would be foolish to defy me. You may be able to perform karate, but it would seem that I must give you some lessons in judo!' He laughed harshly. 'However, first I must teach you another lesson, hmm?'

She couldn't say anything. Some rational part of her mind was impatiently demanding to know what madness had taken hold of her. In hitting out at him with her tongue and her hands, she knew that she had been wounding herself as much as Alvaro. More importantly, the pressure of his weight on her was playing havoc with her senses. Through her own thin clothes she could feel the warmth of his body, the coiled tension of the muscles beneath his suntanned skin

She opened her eyes as the silence lengthened. He was staring down at her, his mouth opening to say something, but no words came. Lyn began to tremble violently, her eyes caught and held by the dawning gleam in his dark eyes. His hands came down to hold her head firmly beneath him and with a sound somewhere between a groan and a laugh he bent his head.

Her lips trembled beneath his, her body limp and yielding under him as she at last realised with total clarity why it was that she had tried to hurt him so viciously, what it was that she had been afraid to admit even to herself. With a desperate hunger she wound her arms about his neck, her shaking fingers burying themselves in his soft black hair as she moved her body convulsively beneath him, aware of nothing but the realisation that she loved this man with all her heart, now and forever.

Reason told her that it was a relationship that could have no future, but rational thought had no place in the emotional drive which now had her in its thrall. The desperate ache deep inside her clamoured for release, and as his fingers lightly unbuttoned and then moved inside her shirt to touch her warm, bare flesh, a small moan of contentment escaped her lips. She knew she ought to feel shame as he exposed her fully to his gaze, but she was aware only of a tremulous, aching excitement as his hands cupped her breasts, his head descending as his mouth moved hungrily over the warm curves whose rosy tips burgeoned and hardened at his erotic touch. Her stomach muscles clenched as she was swept by waves of sensual pleasure, a sensation that rocked her to the very foundations of her soul.

'I want you. *Dios*, how I want you!'

If she had any doubts about his own reaction, they were silenced by the oddly hoarse, thick tone in his voice as his words echoed her own need of him. He raised his head and looked down at her intently, his face reflecting the desire she knew to be in her own, his eyes glittering like polished jet, the dark flush on his face as his mouth parted on an unsteady intake of air.

'Well, *querida*, what am I going to do about you, hmm?' he asked softly. 'If I do not take you to my bed very soon, I will surely become *loco*—and you too, I think,' he added with a brief, twisted smile.

She flushed as his words evoked sensual images of their lovemaking together, trembling in his arms as she wondered if he would be irritated by her lack of experience.

'Yes, it is a terrible thing that I propose,' he muttered harshly, mistaking her quivering fear of the unknown for that of revulsion. 'That I should wish to make love to a woman who is the *afianzada* of my own brother—*Dios!* It is a sin.'

'No!' she cried. 'You don't understand. . . .'

'Ah yes,' he sighed deeply. 'Alas, I do. Only too well. Come,' he said, rolling off her body. 'We must strive to control ourselves. Sweet Mother of God,' he groaned, his voice heavy with self-disgust. 'I am surely too old to be turned from the path of family duty by nothing more than a pretty face!'

Lyn's eyes were blinded by tears as she struggled to do up her shirt. Her dazed mind could hardly bear to contemplate the truth: that all he felt for her was, as he had so succinctly said, a male desire to make love to 'a pretty face'. As her fingers fumbled with her buttons, her only thought was to offer up a heartfelt prayer to her guardian angel that she hadn't openly declared her love. The overwhelming despair she now felt at his rejection of her was bad enough, the shocked amazement with which he would have greeted her words, could only have been unimaginably far worse.

CHAPTER SEVEN

'... TE quiero—*te amo!* Can't you see that I want you—I love you. ...' The singer's voice filled the dark, cavernous nightclub with his mournful song of unrequited love, his words finding a painful echo in Lyn's desolate heart. Staring down at her glass, she fervently wished that she hadn't prevailed upon Ramon to take her out tonight. Maybe, if she was enjoying herself, it wouldn't be too bad. But she wasn't; and when Alvaro found out that she had persuaded Ramon to defy his orders, his wrath would be terrible, falling not just on her head, but on that of the blameless young man, now humming happily in tune with the singer and looking about him as he assessed the local female talent.

'*Che*, Lyn!' he leant over to whisper in her ear. 'I am sure that woman over there is mad for me—what do you think, eh?'

There's no doubt about it, the *machismo* of Mexican men is simply incredible, Lyn thought wryly. Her eyes followed his to where a voluptuous woman of about thirty was sitting alone at a table.

'A woman on her own is most unusual,' he murmured as the song finished and the couples dancing on the small, pocket handkerchief of a space near the band wandered back to their tables. '*Si,*' Ramon said, ordering two more *margaritas* from a passing waiter. 'I think that I will ask her to dance. You do not mind?'

'No, of course not.' She smiled at his young, flushed face. 'Good hunting!'

'Ah, Lyn, what a wonderful girl you are!' he exclaimed with a laugh as he rose and left the table.

112

She could hardly tell him just how relieved she was that he had fallen out of love with her, she thought, almost as easily as he had tumbled into love a few weeks ago. She had done her best to dampen his enthusiastic ardour, and considered his present interest in anything female, and mature women in particular, to be far healthier than hankering after his brother's fiancée. Although, if he ever had the opportunity of setting his eyes on the *real* Marilyn's cleavage, he might well change his mind again!

A gurgle of laughter rose in her throat and she looked down at her *margarita* in consternation. Oh goodness! I've been drinking far too many of these, she told herself sternly as she nevertheless lifted the glass to her lips again. Ramon had warned her that the mixture of tequila, cointreau and lime juice was a lethal one, and she was beginning to see what he meant. Well, it might not be a bad idea to get smashed out of her skull for the first time in her life. It might help to anaesthetise her present, wretched misery, her hopeless yearning for Alvaro's warm embrace.

After her tearful return to the *hacienda*, Lyn had been unable to walk for two days because of the strain she had put on her damaged ankle when rescuing the little girl from the bull. Lying on her bed in stunned despair, she was oblivious of everything except the agony of her aching heart as she struggled to come to terms with Alvaro's rejection. She had been almost unable to comprehend the sheer brutal unfairness of her situation. Just when she had realised that she loved a man with all her heart, only a few moments later he had made it plain that he didn't reciprocate her feelings. Oh yes, he might want to possess her body, but that was all. He had made it quite clear that what he felt was lust, not love. It was just as simple and as heart-breaking as that.

She had desperately tried to conjure up the visions of his past unkind behaviour, his raging fury and arrogance. It was no good. All she could seem to see in her mind's eye was the obverse side of the same coin. His care and concern that his brother Felipe should marry the right woman, so important in a Catholic country which did not recognise divorce. His loving fondness for Carlos and his obvious distress that Mercedes had been too frightened to go to him with her problem; and even his gentle touch as he had cradled the little child in his arms, soothing her fright with soft words before instructing his brother to take her back to the village. Not to mention his care and responsibility for his family who relied so much on him. For the first time she realised what a heavy burden it must be.

You're mad! she told herself again and again. He's a terrible, obnoxious, arrogant man whom you've actively disliked ever since you first met him. Of course he's got some good qualities, no one's all bad. Even Hitler's mother must have been fond of him—but so what? And when that argument failed to sway her weak, inner self, she finally accepted the bitter truth. It didn't matter what he had said or done in the past, she loved the man—for his faults as much as for his virtues.

Desperate unhappiness numbed her heart as she tried to find the courage and resolution to pick up the pieces of her life again. It would mean having to face the living purgatory of Alvaro's constant presence; never being able to get away from his tall, vibrantly masculine figure, and having to face the sight of him and Dolores together.

Dolores! At the thought of the beautiful woman and the relationship Lyn was sure she had with Alvaro, she finally gave way to a heavy storm of bitter tears, writhing in agony as her heated body and mind fought to keep the images of the two lovers at bay.

What Mercedes and Doña Elena thought about the long silent, tearful days she spent in her room, Lyn had no idea. Doña Elena had tried to talk kindly to her, but she hardly heard a word the older woman had said, her mind and body almost smothered by the heavy quilt of her misery.

When, on the third day, Lyn finally summoned up the courage to leave her room, it was to find the servants busily packing at Doña Elena's announcement that the family were going to stay in their house in Monterrey.

'Alvaro is down there at the moment,' she informed Lyn. 'He is very worried, although he does not like to say anything to Mercedes, of course. It seems that Ricardo has completely disappeared.'

'Oh no!' Lyn felt conscience-stricken at having so weakly given in to her own troubles, when those of Mercedes were obviously far worse.

'Sí. Ricardo telephoned Mercedes to say that he was going away for a time, and not to worry if she didn't hear directly from him. He told her that he would contact Alvaro; but while my son has told his sister that all is well and that he has heard from her husband—it is not so.'

'Oh, I . . . I'm so sorry. Is there anything I can do?' Lyn asked, feeling helpless in the face of such a family disaster.

Doña Elena shrugged unhappily. 'Alvaro's agents have lost all trace of Ricardo for the moment, but of course we hope, yes? That is why I have decided to leave and go to Monterrey. We will be on the spot there, and also Mercedes has lots of friends who will be company for her. She is no fool and suspects that all is not well. So, maybe you can help her by keeping Carlos happy and occupied during this time?'

'Yes, of course I will.'

'You are a good, kind girl, my dear Lyn.' Doña Elena looked at the dark shadows beneath the slim girl's unhappy blue eyes, the lines of strain on her pale complexion. It seemed as if she was about to say something more, hesitating for a moment before she gave Lyn a warm smile and turned away to see to the packing.

Bewildered by the speed of events, Lyn found herself, a day later, ensconced in the palatial mansion of the Costillo family, surrounded by acres of lawns, trees and flower beds. Despite the space and luxury, it did not take Lyn long to realise that she was still a prisoner.

The day after they had arrived she took Carlos for a walk around the grounds, finding to her increasing dismay that everywhere they went, they eventually came to a high wall. Attempting the next morning to leave by the massively heavy wrought iron gates at the end of the drive, she was stopped by a guard who stepped smartly out of a small hut. Smiling and courteous, he consulted a list before he gently but firmly refused to open the gates. She realised that he must have telephoned directly back to the house, as on her return she was informed by a servant that Don Alvaro wished to see her in his study.

'How dare you tell your man at the gate that I'm not allowed to leave this place!' she demanded in a blazing fury as she marched into the room.

Alvaro leant back in his chair behind the desk, slowly and deliberately lighting a cigar as he regarded her with unfathomable eyes. It seemed an age before he spoke. 'Why would you think that the conditions of your stay in this house should in any way be different to those back at the *hacienda*, hmm?'

Whereas a week ago the sound of his mocking, sardonic drawl would have been enough to provoke a furious outburst, Lyn now found herself completely tongue-tied, her feet rooted to the floor as she fought to control her emotions. All her good resolutions, all her reasoned arguments had vanished, at the sight of Alvaro's handsome face. She closed her eyes as she was swept by a dizzy, trembling longing for the feel of his strong arms about her.

'I . . . I . . . er . . .' she croaked hoarsely, a hard lump in her throat seemed to be preventing her from saying anything.

'So silent, my dear Lyn?' A slight, humourless smile twisted his lips. 'Very well, I shall make the facts plain to you in the hope that I shall not have to repeat myself again. I have given instructions that you are to be regarded as a guest in this house—a valued guest, I may add. However, I have also made it quite clear, both to my family and the servants, that this house is where you stay until such time as I decide otherwise. Do you understand?'

He took her continued silence for assent. 'Good, I am glad that we understand each other at last.' He gave a short, hard bark of laughter. 'You may take it as a compliment that I had to exercise all my authority to force my stepmother and Ramon to agree to what I have just said. My stepmother appears to believe you can do no wrong, while as for Ramon, he would seem to have fallen deeply in love, no less! Of course, he does not know you as I do, hmm?' he added softly.

Lyn flinched at the disgust she felt sure she could hear in his voice, the humiliating way in which he was addressing her. Surely, if she had any pride at all, she would say something, if only to tell this man exactly what she thought of him? But . . . but what she thought of him—about him—were emotions which she would never be able to put into words, not words that he would be willing to hear. . . .

'Lyn! Are you feeling all right?'

She glanced across the room as he stood up, her heart performing a series of painful somersaults at the concern expressed on his tanned features. Don't be an idiot! she wildly counselled herself. He'd shown the same concern for Carlos, probably more in fact. The echoing silence in the high-ceilinged room, Alvaro's tall, powerful figure—it all suddenly became too much for her to cope with. She knew, with a dreadful certainty, that if she stayed a moment longer she would dissolve into weak, feeble tears. Unconsciously putting up a hand as if to ward off a blow, she turned and fled to the bedroom suite she had been allocated at the other end of the house.

And, since she hadn't seen Alvaro again, that had been that, Lyn thought, gloomily sipping her strong drink and watching Ramon chatting vivaciously as he led the voluptuous woman on to the dance floor. Well, at least he seemed to be enjoying himself. It hadn't exactly been a fun evening for him so far, and if she hadn't been feeling so desperately lonely and unhappy, she would never have tried to persuade Ramon to help her escape for a few hours from her 'prison'.

Irritably waving away a man who was approaching her table, clearly having assumed that a woman sitting alone was fair game, she tried to think about her future. She had been so sunk in misery about her non-existent relationship with Alvaro that she had given little or no thought to what was happening elsewhere. Specifically, what on earth were Marilyn and Larry Wilde doing? They must surely have found out by now that she had disappeared from the hospital, but although she scanned the English-speaking newspapers each day, she had found no snippets of news about either Marilyn or the film.

The scraping of a chair beside her cut into her thoughts. Oh, for heaven's sake! Not another man thinking he was God's gift to women? She turned to tell the interloper to remove himself, in what little Spanish she possessed, and nearly died with fright as she found herself looking into the dark, angry eyes of Alvaro.

Trembling with shock, she gazed at the man who had so suddenly appeared from nowhere like the demon king in a pantomime. All he needs is a cloud of green smoke, she thought almost hysterically, viewing his tall, authoritative figure dressed in an immaculately cut dinner suit. Among the other customers of the nightclub his aristocratic elegance made him stand out like some sleek raven amidst a crowd of dusty sparrows. Lyn blushed as his eyes swept over her pale apricot chiffon dress which she had been lent by Mercedes. She was distractingly aware of his gaze resting on the full curves of her breasts displayed by the low-cut bodice.

'What ... what are you doing here?' she asked breathlessly.

'*Dios!*' he ground out in exasperation. 'Isn't it enough that I have to worry about my sister and her missing husband, without having to search all over this town for you!'

'Please ... please don't be too cross, Alvaro. It's not Ramon's fault,' she assured him nervously. 'It was all my idea. I ... I persuaded him to help me leave the house. He ...'

'Do you think that I don't know that!' he snorted angrily.

'He is a good boy, but very young and therefore putty in experienced hands such as yours. Is it not enough for you that you have captured Felipe, that you must also have Ramon?'

'Oh, for goodness sake, don't be so ridiculous! Anyway, why should you care, especially since you've got *dear*, *darling* Dolores climbing all over you?' She laughed wildly as she tossed back her almost full glass, choking and spluttering as the fiery liquid exploded in her stomach, her ears ringing with Alvaro's cynical laugh—damn him!

'That will teach you to drink more carefully,' he grinned, his exasperated anger seeming to have vanished as suddenly as he himself had appeared in the nightclub.

When she managed to catch a breath, Lyn attempted

to set the record straight. She knew it was a waste of time, but at least she must try.

'Why don't you forget Felipe for a moment, and just look at Ramon?' She pointed at his brother's figure entwined with his partner on the dance floor. 'Yes, of course he decided he was in love with me, up at the *hacienda*. Other than Miguel's wife and Mercedes, I was just about the only woman under fifty, for heaven's sake! However, by the time he had been back here in Monterrey for two days, he'd already started to play the field, and by tomorrow morning he will undoubtedly be in love with that woman he's dancing with!'

She sighed as she looked at the tight, closed expression on his face which gave her no clue as to what he was thinking. 'Can't you understand that he's going to fall in and out of love every week for the next two years, at least?'

'We will leave the subject of Ramon. Maybe, instead you can tell me just what *you* are doing here, in this most unsuitable of places, and why you defied my orders for you to stay in the house, hmm?' Once again there was no expression in either his face or his voice to give her a clue as to what he was thinking.

Lyn tried to still her trembling hands by clasping them tightly together in her lap. 'You may not want the truth, but I'm going to tell you all the same,' she said with what little defiance she was able to muster. 'I was so unhappy and lonely and . . . and miserable, that I thought I'd die if I didn't get out—away for a few hours at least. And I . . . I don't need you to tell me that it has all been a ghastly mistake—because I know that, OK?' She looked away, taking in the tawdry furnishings, the people who couldn't contain their drink and lay sprawled across the tables in a drunken stupor. 'You're quite . . . quite right,' she wrinkled her nose. 'This is an unsuitable place, really horrid in fact.'

Alvaro surprised her by laughing again. 'Never mind,

querida, there are far worse places than this, believe me!' He stood up and bent to help her rise. Thinking that he was now about to take her home, she allowed him to lead her away from the table, blinking in confusion as he walked towards the dance floor, not the doorway.

'This isn't the way out,' she told him.

'No, of course not. I wish to have a word with my brother.'

'Oh, please don't be too hard on him . . .' she began before she breathlessly realised he was placing his arms about her figure.

'W-what . . .?'

He sighed. 'Really, Lyn, you surely can't be expecting me to march through that crowd? It is obvious that we must dance, hmm?'

'Well . . . yes, I . . . I suppose so . . .' she murmured, the close contact with his tall elegant figure causing her stomach to knot with tension. She nervously tried to hold herself stiffly away from him, but another couple barged into the back of her, pushing her firmly into close contact with his hard body. By the time she had recovered from the collision, his arms were lightly but firmly restraining her from moving away.

She could only be profoundly thankful for the dim light which hid the tide of crimson she could feel covering her face, nervous tremors of uncontrollable excitement running up and down her spine at the feel of his figure so close to hers. The musky scent of his cologne filled her nostrils as he placed his cheek next to hers, the warmth of his tanned skin through the thin silk of his shirt causing her heart to thud painfully as he drew her closer and closer to him.

'We . . . we aren't moving towards Ramon . . .' she gasped, trying and failing to control the rising tide of desire which flowed through her trembling body.

'I said I wished to have a word with my brother. I did

not say exactly when,' he murmured, brushing his warm lips across her temple. She shivered at his touch, swiftly losing any ability to think clearly as he gently trailed his mouth across her cheek to softly touch the corner of her lips.

At that moment the band finished playing a dance tune, and blew a fanfare to announce the arrival of the comedian, who ran on to the small stage to a smattering of applause.

Saved by a trumpet! Lyn thought hysterically as Alvaro lifted his head. He nodded across the floor at Ramon, who took his partner back to her table before approaching his brother with a guilty look on his face. Alvaro stood with his arms still firmly about Lyn's blushing figure as the two exchanged some sentences in Spanish, before Ramon laughed, slapped Alvaro on the back and winked at Lyn before striding away.

'What . . . what did you say to Ramon?' she queried huskily as he led her out of the door.

Alvaro shrugged, tossing a coin to the man guarding his car outside the nightclub. Opening the passenger door of what she was amazed to see was the long body of an Aston Martin Saloon, he merely commented, 'I decided to take heed of your remarks, earlier. You are very likely right, and Ramon will come to no harm with that woman.' He turned the ignition key, and they roared away from the kerb with a powerful thrust from the car's V8 engine.

During the short, silent journey Lyn desperately tried to collect her scattered wits, and by the time they arrived at the house, she had managed to find a small measure of composure. Leading her into the hall, he nodded towards the closed door of his study. 'Would you care for a drink?' he asked blandly.

'Oh, no! I . . . I mean, I'm rather tired, and I . . . I think that. . . .'

Her words were interrupted by the door of the study being thrown open and the sudden appearance in the doorway of a tall, slim man whose handsome features were creased into a worried frown.

'*Dios gracias . . .!*' He burst out, before he noticed Lyn. Giving her a brief, puzzled glance, he turned back to address Alvaro. 'I cannot take any more! It is not right that you should ask it of me – you must see that? First you part me from my beloved *afianzada*, and now, when my sister needs all the help she can get, you expect me to stay in Spain. It is not right, it is not reasonable, and I have decided to come home—say what you will!' he added defiantly.

Bewildered, still feeling nervously strung up and confused by the events of the evening, Lyn glanced at Alvaro. She was surprised to see him give a weary shrug, his dark eyes gazing intently into hers before they were shrouded by his heavy eyelids as he turned back to the strange man.

'Ah well,' he sighed heavily. 'It seems that I must accept defeat. If you really love each other so much, who am I to stand in your way, Felipe.'

'*Felipe . . .?*' Lyn gasped, staring at the stranger.

'Who is this woman?' Felipe asked, looking at her with equal bewilderment.

Alvaro gave a bitter laugh. 'Have you forgotten her so soon? What has happened to the great love you have been talking about for the last six months, eh?'

'But—but this is not my Marilyn! How could you think so?' Felipe demanded of his brother in astonishment.

'*What!*' Alvaro spun on his heels, glaring at Lyn as if unable to believe his ears.

Lyn's mouth was suddenly dry with tension. 'I told you! I . . . I told you at the hospital that . . . that I wasn't Marilyn. But you . . . you wouldn't listen. My . . . my name is Lynette Harris and . . . and I wish I'd never been born!' she wailed, suddenly overcome by all the tensions of the last weeks.

'Ah, no!' It was Felipe who expressed concern. Felipe who strode quickly over to place an arm about the tearful figure of the girl and lead her gently into the study, before seating her down in a comfortable chair. Despite the sobs which wracked her slight figure, she noticed that Alvaro said nothing. He just stood in the doorway, staring at her as if he was seeing a ghost.

'Very well,' he said at last in a cold voice. 'If you are not Marilyn, what were you doing at that hospital? Why did they think that you were Marilyn Thorne? And finally, the most interesting question of all: Where is Marilyn?'

Lyn sniffed, fishing in her handbag for a handkerchief to blow her nose. 'I . . . I was Marilyn's stand-in for the film, and I also performed the stunts. That . . . that's my job,' she explained to Felipe. 'As it turned out, I had to take Marilyn's place for much of the location work when she fell ill with Montezuma's revenge. . . .'

'It will be nothing to *my* revenge when I have finally managed to sort this matter out!' growled Alvaro as she fell silent. 'Come on, tell us the rest,' he demanded.

'Well, I did a dangerous stunt and . . . and it all went wrong. I woke up in the hospital to find that because I'd been doing some of Marilyn's acting for her, they all thought I was her . . . if you see what I mean,' she added wearily.

'So why didn't you tell the hospital the truth?'

'What in the hell is this—the Spanish inquisition?' she cried, exhausted by the rapid fire of his questions.

'Ah, you poor girl,' Felipe murmured, getting up to pour her a stiff whisky and soda, studiously ignoring Alvaro's sour comment that Lyn had obviously had quite enough to drink that night already.

The strong liquor made her feel more confident. 'I woke up in the hospital to find I had nothing on me to prove who I was. I had been filming in costume, so I wasn't even wearing a watch, for heaven's sake. And

... and if you think I had the forethought to tuck a passport down my blouse before I jumped off that cliff—then you must be mad!'

Alvaro snorted in exasperation. '*Sí, Sí*, of course I understand. But there must have been some way. . . .'

'There wasn't!' she snapped. 'And believe me, I certainly tried to think of one! The doctor was totally convinced I had amnesia. Moreover, it was the last day of filming on location and all the crew would have gone back to the United States. If you knew the film business,' she added swiftly, as he seemed about to argue the point, 'you'd know that the only thing that matters is the budget for the movie. I already knew that they had overspent their allocation of funds, so it was a certainty that they would have decamped back to the studios as fast as possible.'

There was a pause as the two men digested what she had said. 'Very well,' Alvaro said at last. 'I will accept what you say. . . .'

'Oh great! Simply fantastic!' she fumed. 'I just *love* your profuse apology for dragging me halfway across this country, shouting and swearing at me for the last weeks, accusing me of being a loose woman and intimate with half the men in America. . . .'

'What!' Felipe looked angrily at Alvaro. 'Did you dare suggest that my beloved. . . .'

'*Por Dios*, Felipe! You know my views on your fiancée – I've told you enough times!'

'But to accuse this poor girl of such a thing!'

'Yes, well. . . .'

Lyn's blue eyes widened. Almost unbelievably, it looked as if Alvaro was blushing! And so he ought, she thought, recalling some of the things he had said to her. Her reverie was interrupted by Felipe jumping to his feet and striding distractedly about the room.

'But where . . . where is my Marilyn?' He demanded of both his brother and Lyn.

'A very good question,' Alvaro agreed, turning to stare intently at her flushed face. 'Well?'

'Well, what?' she parried, desperately trying to think of what to say.

'Don't prevaricate!' he snapped angrily. 'You know very well where she is.'

'No, I don't. Not exactly, anyway,' she temporised, suddenly deciding that she hadn't gone through the past weeks masquerading as Marilyn, to throw it all away now. Felipe was obviously madly in love with the film star, certainly strongly enough to defy his brother and return from Spain against Alvaro's express orders. Why shouldn't they have a chance of happiness?

' *"Not exactly"*,' mimicked Alvaro savagely. 'That won't do, Lyn and you know it!'

'It's the literal truth, I promise you,' she assured him with all the sincerity at her command. 'All I know is that Marilyn had to attend to ... er ... to urgent family business. No,' she answered Felipe. 'I don't know where her home is, or indeed where her parents live. But I do know that she is due to be in Mexico City very soon.'

The two brothers conferred earnestly together in Spanish, and Lyn took the opportunity to slip quietly out of the room.

Later, as she stood on the balcony of her bedroom, looking down at the lights of Monterrey spread out before her, she realised that her life with the Costillo family had come to an end. She really ought to be packing, instead of standing here, gazing out into the warm darkness of the Mexican night. But what had she to pack? She had arrived with nothing but the hospital shift, and that had been thrown away weeks ago. Everything she wore, even her toothbrush had been provided by Alvaro's family.

There was a tight knot of misery in her stomach and she felt slightly sick at the knowledge she might not see

Alvaro again before she left. But in fact, she thought wearily, it might be just as well if she made a point of *not* seeing him again. There was no point in hurting herself any further, and his life was here with his family—and with Dolores.

Resolutely, she tried to turn her thoughts away from the man she loved as she reviewed the events of the last hour. At least she had done what she could for Marilyn. If Felipe spent his time trying to track her down in Mexico City, or contacted the studios to try and find out details of her whereabouts, it would, if necessary, give the film star sufficient time to complete her Las Vegas divorce. Privately, Lyn thought that Marilyn ought to tell Felipe about her past, trusting in his love to overcome all difficulties.

Lyn felt a slight breeze on her cheek and the sound of a door opening and closing in the dark room behind her. Startled, almost not believing her ears, she moved back into the bedroom and switched on a small table light which softly illuminated the room with its dim glow.

She gasped nervously as she saw Alvaro standing by the closed door. He had discarded his dinner jacket and tie, and was wearing only a silk shirt and dark trousers. His shirt was half unbuttoned and she could plainly see the dark hairs on the tanned skin of his broad chest.

'What ... what do you want?' she said, still endeavouring to recover from the shock of his silent entry.

He remained standing where he was, regarding her intently. 'I wanted—I had to see you. We have some unfinished business to conclude,' he replied tautly.

'But I ... I've told you all there is to know. . . .' She was only too well aware of the jerky breathiness of her voice and wished that she could sound cool and indifferent.

'I am not referring to the conversation we both had with my brother.'

Lyn swallowed·hard. 'Well, in that case I . . . er . . . I don't know what you are talking about.' She blushed a deep red as she suddenly realised that she was wearing the diaphanous nightgown she had been given by Mercedes. Crossing her arms protectively over her breasts, she raised her head defiantly.

'I know this is your house, but for the moment I have the use of this room, and that gives me the right to demand that you leave it!'

'Keep your voice down!' commanded Alvaro tersely. 'Surely you don't want the whole household to hear our conversation?'

'As far as I'm concerned there will be no conversation,' she retorted in a low voice, turning away to go and lean out over the balcony, grateful for the cool breeze which fanned her flushed cheeks.

Felipe must be still up, she thought as she caught the faints strains of some music being played downstairs. It was such a beautiful night with the brilliant stars shining like a diamond necklace against a sky of dark blue velvet. The scent of the flowers down below in the garden drifted up with the night air, and she wondered dreamily how anyone could remain immune on such an evening of enchantment. It was surely a night for lovers. A night made for love and sweet surrender, not for arguments and angry words. If only, if only she had the courage to turn to Alvaro, to wind her arms about his dark head and tell him that she loved him. . . .

And then he was standing behind her, his hands lightly grasping her slim waist. 'I too have no interest in conversation,' he said thickly, drawing her trembling body back against his hard figure, his hands moving slowly upwards to caress her full breasts and the nipples which leapt to life, hardening beneath his erotic touch.

'No . . .!' she gasped, her body trembling violently as she felt herself weakly losing all control.

'*Dios!*' he breathed, turning her gently to face him. 'Don't you understand how I have been tortured by my thoughts? Night and day they have given me no peace.'

'Thoughts . . .?' she whispered, running her tongue over lips that were suddenly dry.

'Thoughts of making love to you,' he murmured thickly, sliding an arm about her waist, his other hand gently brushing the hair away from her brow. 'I have wanted you since the first day I saw you in that hospital, surely you know that? I want you,' he groaned, breathing swiftly and unsteadily. '*Por Dios!* I must have you . . .!'

Lyn knew she was helplessly lost as she felt the muscled strength of his firm body against her quivering figure. But still she tried to cling to sanity.

'It's wrong . . .' she gasped. 'It's only lust. . . .'

'Lust? Then so be it . . .!' he said roughly as he bent his head, his mouth caressing her neck before trailing up to seek her lips. '*Te quiero, te quiero,*' he murmured, softly and delicately exploring the outline of her lips with a tenderly sensual, delicate touch that made her senses reel. She felt as if she was drowning, his warm, firm mouth becoming more insistent, moving over her lips and forcing them apart. She was swept by a raging, pulsating storm of desire as his tongue explored the inner softness of her mouth, and she melted in his arms with complete abandon.

His body shook with a convulsive shudder as she surrendered her will to his. Sweeping her up in his arms, he carried her swiftly over to the large bed. She felt as if she was lost in a dream, having no shame as Alvaro gently drew the thin silk nightgown from her trembling figure, and even revelling in the fiery gleam from his eyes as he gazed down at her naked body. Almost instinctively she reached up to unfasten the remaining buttons of his shirt, pressing her lips against the rough hairs of his chest and drawing a hoarse groan from deep in his throat as his lips and hands moved urgently over her body.

'*Dios*, how beautiful you are!' he told her huskily as he paused to wrench off his clothes. 'I have dreamed of nothing but possessing your lovely, pale body, but my dreams were but frustrating nightmares, until now. . . .' He moved to cover her with his hard frame.

'I . . . I don't know what to do . . . I've never . . .' her softly breathed words were so indistinct as to be barely audible.

'I am your first man?' he asked gently, giving a soft, low laugh of delight when she blushed and nodded silently.

'Ah, my little one, you need have no fear. I will lead you carefully to the delights of the flesh. Trust me, hmm?'

They were almost the last words she heard as she sank beneath wave after wave of increasing pleasure. There was no room for thoughts of right or wrong, just the overpowering urgency of her need for him. . . .

CHAPTER EIGHT

LYN was awakened the next morning by Carlos bouncing up and down on the end of her bed. Sleepily opening her eyes, it was some time before she recalled the previous night's events. Panic-stricken, she rolled swiftly over to look at the other side of the bed, sighing with relief when she saw that there was no evidence of Alvaro's occupation, other than a red rose which lay on the pillow where his head had been. Picking up the rose, which had obviously been taken from those twining about the iron balcony outside her room, she gazed blindly down at the soft, crimson petals.

'*Tia* Lyn!' Carlos bounced excitedly. 'You must hurry up and get dressed. *Tio* Felipe is going to take me shopping to choose a present for my mama. It is her birthday next week.'

Lyn sighed deeply and struggled into a sitting position, holding the sheet close to her naked body as she tried to focus her eyes on the small jewelled clock across the room. It was ten o'clock—far later than she normally slept.

'You . . . you won't need me if you are going with your uncle,' she murmured, her mind beginning to fill with memories of the night she had spent in Alvaro's arms.

'But yes! *Tio* Felipe was very cross with *Tio* Alvaro at breakfast early this morning. *Tio* Felipe said you had been treated very badly. He said we are to take you out with us. So please,' he begged, 'do hurry up!'

Lyn closed her eyes as she tried to think what to do. In the first place, she had no money to go shopping; and in fact, what she ought to do was to begin

131

organising her departure from this house. Despite what had happened last night between Alvaro and herself it would be incredibly foolish of her to build any hopes and dreams on such a foundation. No, she must leave, and as quickly as she could. But the thought of discussing the matter with Alvaro was ... was unbearable. Maybe Felipe would be able to help her?

'Yes, all right, Carlos.' She smiled wanly at the child as he bounced off the bed. 'Tell your uncle that I ... I will be down as soon as I've got dressed.'

Later, as she and Carlos gazed in a shop window, admiring the local leather work while Felipe completed a purchase inside, Lyn congratulated herself on her decision to come out with Carlos and his uncle. Felipe had said that he would take them for a cup of coffee at the Gran Ancira Hotel on the corner of the Plaza Hidalgo, which lay just a few yards away from where they were shopping. She would be able to have a quiet word with him there, and hopefully enlist his help in organising her departure. . . .

Her complacent thoughts were sharply interrupted by a frightened cry from Carlos and she spun around to see him kicking and struggling as he was being dragged by two men towards a large black limousine. Gasping with disbelief, she ran swiftly towards him across the wide pavement, shouting angrily and yelling for help. Despite the commotion, none of the other shoppers in the Plaza seemed to understand what was happening as she caught hold of one man's arm and began frantically kicking his shins.

'Help ...!' she screamed as loudly as she could, reeling from a blow on her back as she locked her arms about Carlos' small figure. She felt herself falling to the ground, before she and the child were bodily picked up and thrown into the back of the car.

'For God's sake, Joe! Let's get out of here!' one of the men shouted as he thrust himself into the car beside her, while the other man jumped into the driving seat, slamming his foot down on the throttle and the car roared away down the street. With dazed eyes, the last thing Lyn saw was Felipe's white, shocked face as he dashed out of the shop, before she felt a blow on the back of her head, and knew no more.

She came to in darkness. An enveloping, thick, and stifling darkness caused by something which felt rough against her face as she tried to raise her head. Feeling sick and dizzy, she lapsed back into the swirling mists which clouded her brain, slowly resurfacing as she realised that she could feel motion beneath her, and something at the back of her mind insisting that she must wake up. Moving cautiously, she realised she was on the floor of what seemed to be a car, a blanket or some dark material having been placed over her head and body. Why? Gradually her muzzy brain cleared sufficiently for her to recall the men snatching Carlos, and Felipe's horrified face as they had been driven away. She almost blacked out again at the realisation that she and Carlos had been kidnapped!

Struggling with the blanket, she cried out as she received a vicious kick in her stomach. 'Keep still!' a disembodied, hoarse voice commanded from somewhere above her prone figure. 'You'd better keep still, or I'll hit you harder next time—OK?'

There was little she could do, but lie on the floor of the car, battling against waves of sickness and worry about what had happened to Carlos. Was he in the car with her? She tried to concentrate, but could hear nothing other than some indistinct muttering between the two men. She had no idea of the time she lay there, she was only aware of the car being swung this way and that, the wheels squealing as they rounded one sharp corner after another. At last they came to a halt, and still covered by the dark blanket, she was dragged out of the car.

Minutes later she stood blinking rapidly beneath the hard brilliance of neon lights. She was standing in what appeared to be a large garage, her arms firmly held by one of the men as the other kidnapper dragged Carlos' body from the car. His small eyes were closed, his face chalky white as he lay limply in the man's arms.

'You've killed him!' she screamed, sobbing with anger and fright. 'You murderers! You're nothing but . . . agh!' she gasped, reeling from a hard slap on her cheek.

'You just shut your mouth, sister, OK?' The man holding her arm pushed his craggy face into hers. 'One more peep out of you, and it's curtains! Get the message?' He leered evilly as she gazed back at him in terror, before he swiftly clasped her hands behind her back, tying them with some rope he took from his pocket. 'OK, Joe, how's the kid?'

'He's fine,' the other man replied laconically as he placed Carlos' body on a pile of rags by a work bench. 'I only gave him a whiff of the chloroform, just like you said to, Lew.'

Lew, the man beside her, merely grunted, pushing her back against the car and telling her not to move—or else! Resting her head against the cold steel of the car roof, she watched with glazed eyes as he went over to a phone by the wall, dialled a number and spoke briefly before replacing the receiver and going over to have a look at Carlos.

The passing time seemed like eternity, while the men just stood chatting idly to each other, obviously waiting for someone, or something to happen. Never, in all her life, had Lyn felt so frightened. Her knees were knocking with terror, her numbed mind filled with nameless, dreadful fears of what could be going to happen to her and Carlos. Her body broke out into a cold sweat and if she hadn't had the car to lean against she would have slumped to the floor.

Suddenly, there was a noise of an engine outside, and

the man called Lew ran to open the overhead garage door, allowing a large, white Mercedes Benz to draw inside. The man who got slowly out of the car was very different from those who had kidnapped Lyn and Carlos. Immaculately dressed in a pale grey suit, his hands covered in gold rings, he was obviously a Latin American. Just as his henchmen, from their accents and style of dress, looked like what she was to learn they were—American gangsters.

'What is she doing here?' the new arrival demanded in a heavily accented voice. 'You made no mention of a woman on the phone.'

'No, Boss. It seemed well, a better idea to tell you in person. You see, she kinda ran up and grabbed the kid, and with all the noise she was making, it seemed easier to bring her along—know what I mean?'

Lyn looked up to see herself being surveyed by the man's cold, black eyes. If he's organised this kidnapping, we've had it! she found herself thinking as he ran his icy gaze up and down her figure.

'Take her out the back and shoot her,' he commanded, almost as if he was calmly ordering a new suit, she thought numbly. It was only when Lew grasped her arm that her brain cleared and she knew she must fight for her life, if only for Carlos' sake.

'You . . . you would be very foolish to kill me,' she said as calmly as she could, bitterly aware of the tremulous wobble in her voice.

'You are not a member of the Costillo family, so why should I care one way or another what happens to you?' the man said slowly.

He knows the family, so this is *definitely* a kidnapping! she thought swiftly. And I've got to stay with Carlos somehow. . . . 'I'm . . . er . . . I'm the child's nanny,' she improvised wildly. 'His English nanny and . . . and you will need me to look after him, won't you? I mean . . . he's going to be very sick when he wakes up from whatever it is you have given him, isn't he?' She pushed her point home, praying that they hadn't already made arrangements for a woman to look after Carlos.

'I don't suppose these gentlemen here,' she gestured scornfully to Lew and Joe, 'I don't imagine they will appreciate having to clear up the mess. When children are sick, they are *very* sick,' she added firmly, as though she knew what she was talking about.

'Yeah, Boss, the dame's gotta point.'

To her astonishment, the boss of the kidnappers threw back his head and roared with laughter. 'Rule Britannia, eh? Well, why not?' He shrugged. 'It matters very little whether we dispose of you now or later, and as you have said, you may prove to be useful.' He turned to Lew, who seemed to be the senior of the two men. 'Take them to the place as arranged. I will complete the business here and join you tomorrow. *Sí?*'

'Yeah, sure Boss.'

They waited until the man had reversed his white car out of the garage, before dragging Lyn over to a plain grey van. Opening the back doors, Lew thrust her inside as Joe came over carrying Carlos, placing him beside her on the hard floor of the vehicle.

'Get the blanket you had over my head,' she snapped without thinking. 'How on earth do you expect the child to be comfortable like that?'

'I'd keep quiet, sister, if I was you,' Lew warned roughly. 'Just remember you're living on borrowed time, huh?' Nevertheless, she saw him jerk his head at Joe who reappeared with the blanket. Feeling ridiculously cheered by her small victory, she watched as the doors were slammed and she and the little boy were left in the Stygian darkness.

It seemed as if the van had been travelling for ever. Lyn's body was soon a mass of bruises, the ropes biting cruelly into the wrists of the hands tied behind her back, and which she couldn't use to prevent herself from banging against the side of the vehicle. After a while the van seemed to be maintaining a steady course, and she was trying to ignore her aching arms, when she heard Carlos begin to stir. He slowly returned to consciousness, crying out in fear as he found himself in darkness.

'It's all right, darling. I'm here,' she called and a moment later he clambered over to lie with his head in her lap, shaking with fright and complaining of a bad headache.

She waited until his mind had cleared and then she gave him an edited version of what was happening to them. 'Your uncle Alvaro will rescue us very soon,' she assured him brightly, although how that was to happen she had no idea. However, if she wasn't to be killed immediately on her arrival at their destination, she must get him to back up her story that she was his nanny. Leaving out the dire threats to her life, she told him that he must support what she had said, or they wouldn't let her stay with him. Carlos fervently agreed to do so, clearly the thought of being left on his own was a terrifying one.

Eventually, he fell asleep on her lap, and she was left to think of all the terrible things that could happen to them, and probably would. If she hadn't had Carlos to worry about, she realised, she would have been a shuddering mass of hysteria by now. But since she had managed to hang on to her sanity, although only just, she must try and make some plans of escape. But what and how, she had not the slightest notion.

Despite her discomfort, she was almost nodding off to sleep when she suddenly remembered a film on which she had worked last year. It had been a thriller, concerned with the kidnapping of a blonde heroine for whom she was the stand-in, as well as performing a complicated stunt car chase. The director had engaged the services of a retired FBI man to check the kidnap details, and during the long stretches of time between takes he had told her stories of his past life, which she found fascinating. One of the things he had said came back to her now.

'These directors, they like to build up the tension. But in my experience, if a kidnap victim doesn't start to get psychologically on top of the perpetrators right away, or try to escape as soon as possible, then they very seldom make it back alive.'

Lyn had been surprised, since she had assumed that giving kidnappers no trouble was the route to a safe return.

'Nope,' he had stated firmly. 'After a while the bad guys have got themselves organised, and had plenty of time to realise that kidnapping is a federal offence; which means a life stretch in jail if they get caught. The victims, well, they sort of grow numb as time goes by, and stop thinking for themselves. Believe me, kid. If anything ever happens to you, keep your brains working and do everything you can to help yourself as soon as possible. Leave messages where you can, and shout and scream blue murder. While the guys are still sorting things out and hoping for the money, you've got a chance.'

What he had said now gave Lyn a lot to think about, and she passed the time making complicated plans, only to discard them as hopelessly impractical. Nevertheless, as the FBI man had said, it was helping to keep her brain active and if she kept her wits about her, she might be able to seize any opportunity which came her way.

The van came to a halt at last, and there was silence as the driver cut the engine. The back doors of the van were opened, and she blinked at the sudden rush of daylight.

'We're just getting some gas for the tank,' Lew

informed her as Carlos sat up, rubbing his eyes. 'The boy seems OK,' he added beginning to shut the doors again.

'Oh please!' she called. 'Can we . . . can we use the toilet? The boy is feeling sick, and. . . .'

'Well, I don't know.'

'Where can we run to, for heaven's sake?' she retorted. 'Of course, if you don't mind having to clear up the back of this van after the child. . . .'

'OK, OK, but no tricks, you hear.' He helped Carlos out, who remembered her instructions and gripped his tummy, groaned realistically as Lew reached inside to untie her hands, which she realised were completely numb. 'I'll be with you all the way and I've got a gun, so don't try anything,' he hissed in warning as he lead her and Carlos around the side of the gas station to a small annexe, walking inside the toilet with them.

Pushing Carlos' head down in a basin, she turned angrily on the man. 'There are no windows in here, so why don't you wait outside? You can easily stop anyone coming in if you want to. If you stay in here, you're going to be in a fix if a woman should suddenly come in, aren't you?'

Lew shrugged, cast one look around the small room and then left.

'Quick! Turn out your pockets, Carlos, we haven't a moment to lose,' she demanded urgently.

Gazing at her in mystification, he did as he was told. There, to her great relief, amidst some stones, string, two boiled sweets and what looked like a dead snail, was the stub of a pencil.

'Good boy!' she said, excitement shaking her voice as she pulled him into a cubicle and shut the door. 'My hands are too numb, so I want you to write on that door – in Spanish, and in your biggest and best printing. OK?'

'Sí, tía Lyn.' Carlos, who was recovering remarkably

fast from his ordeal, looked pleased at being allowed to perform some graffiti, and not be scolded for doing so.

'I want you to write: "Attention! A large reward will be paid to the first person who rings . . ." Do you know the telephone number of the house in Monterrey?' she asked, with sudden dread that he wouldn't. As he nodded and said the number, she asked him to write it down. 'Now add, that your uncle, Don Alvaro will pay a lot of money for information about a small boy being kidnapped. And write underneath that this is not a joke, but a very serious matter of kidnapping— underline that, Carlos.'

Lew banged on the outside door. Desperately she flushed the toilet, and then dragged Carlos out of the cubicle. 'Don't say a word,' she warned him as Lew entered.

'We are just coming,' she muttered hurriedly. 'The little boy isn't at all well.'

Taking no notice of her words, Lew looked around the room, opening the doors of the cubicles. Lyn's heart was in her mouth, but she breathed again as he didn't think of looking on the back of the cubicle doors.

'OK. Let's go,' he said, issuing them out before him and back to the van. He made to tie her up again, but when she pointed out that she wished to hold the small boy, and in any case she couldn't open the doors from the inside, Lew shrugged and allowed her to scramble in unfettered.

Later that night as she lay on her thin, smelly mattress, listening to Carlos' snores beside her, Lyn's tired mind was full of the scattered images of their arrival in the evening at what had appeared, in the bad light, to be an old mining camp. She and Carlos had been given no time to look around as they were hustled into a large old building and taken up to the second floor, before being locked into a room with bars on the one small window. Two tin plates containing beans and a jug of water had been brought up by Joe, and that had been the last time they had contact with their kidnappers.

Lyn knew she ought to be pacing the room, looking for means of escape, but she was too weary for the moment to do anything. Lying here in the dark, all she could think about was Alvaro. So much, so many terrible things had happened today, that the events of the previous evening seemed somehow to have taken place in another time—almost on another planet. The painful yet delicious recollections of Alvaro's love-making were all she had to cling to; the only point of sanity amidst her sordid surroundings and the blood-chilling, haunting fear of her likely fate at the hands of these evil men.

She trembled as she realised that she had undoubtedly been a fool, allowing Alvaro to make love to her when she knew in her heart that it meant nothing to him but a sexual experience. It was just the enchantment of the night, she told herself desperately, remembering the softly soothing yet arousing feel of his hands on her body. She had been completely lost beneath his mastery of her emotions, the experienced touch of the virtuoso as he played on each sensitive spot to its ultimate sensual pitch. As he had promised, he exercised complete control over his own urges as moment by moment he had led her gently from one erotic sensation to another. Gasping and moaning beneath his mouth and hands, she thought she would die of ecstacy.

'*Que hermosa!* So beautiful, *mi bella amada* ...' he breathed against her trembling flesh. 'So lovely and unawakened, like a fresh rose bud. . . .' His hands and mouth moved down over her body more urgently, the aching sensations he evoked becoming almost unbearable. 'Your skin tastes like nectar, and I want—I must taste every inch. . . .'

Almost fainting with delight, she found that she was

lost to all time and place, and that if she had any virginal inhibitions they had been left behind long ago; her only wish, her only desire being to please Alvaro as he was pleasing her. Her fingers slid down the tanned length of his body, feeling the hard bones of his spine, the taut muscles of his hips, as she revelled in his deep groan at her sensual touch. 'Ah no, *querida* . . .' he protested, as completely swept along on a tide of deep passion, she touched him as intimately as he had touched her, destroying the last remnants of his self control. And then, she too was lost as the heated pressure of his thighs ignited a fire that spread throughout her quivering body. She thought she would surely go mad, that her longing for complete fulfilment was more than she could bear until at last, crying out at his shuddering thrust, she welcomed the pain and the pleasure as she lost complete touch with reality. He seemed to be carrying her far beyond the universe, to the stars and on to infinity, where nothing existed but the fierce waves of unimaginable pleasure. A pleasure that spiralled and exploded, leaving her to free-fall through the stratosphere as she slowly glided down to earth and into a deep sleep, held closely within his warm embrace.

Amidst the horror of her present situation that memory was all she had to cling to, Lyn thought, her body trembling at the sweet recollections of the night before. What was Alvaro doing now? Was he pacing up and down his study, conferring with Felipe about the loss of Carlos and herself? Maybe the ransom note had already been delivered. How would he react? And was he, too, lying in the darkness thinking about their night of passion? Lyn's body began to shake, growing cold and clammy with fear as she realised that not only had she not seen Alvaro since last night, but if the evil men who were keeping her and Carlos captive had their way, she might never—ever—see him again. The dreadful grief and desolation which flooded her mind at such a thought, proved too much to bear. For the first time since the nightmare events had begun on the sunny streets of Monterrey, tears filled her eyes and she buried her head in the mattress as deep, heartbreaking sobs racked her slim frame.

Woken next morning by the entry of Joe with two tin mugs of coffee and some hard rolls, Lyn and Carlos tidied themselves up as much as they could. It was Carlos who found the small windowless room off their bedroom, which contained a toilet and a small hand basin. Determined not to let their standards slip, she bullied Carlos into washing properly, and did the same herself, brushing down her crumpled dress, and trying to comb his dark hair with her fingers. And then there was nothing to do but face the long boredom of the day.

Lyn had woken from her tearful night, coldly and implacably determined not to become inactive, not to allow themselves to become numb and apathetic with despair. Accordingly, she set Carlos to think about the ways and means that he could defend himself, if necessary. It was he, in fact, who came up with the idea of taking off his socks and filling them up with earth to use as a sandbag. 'Not bad,' she said, with a smile of encouragement. 'But we'll have to get hold of some earth first. Keep thinking along those lines and we might come up with something.'

They explored every inch of the room, and apart from thinking that with some matches she could use the stuffing of the mattresses to create a fire, neither of them found anything useful. It wasn't until after a late lunch of the same beans as they had eaten last night, that Carlos made a discovery.

'*Tia* Lyn!' he called urgently from the small toilet. She ran in to see what was wrong, and found him bending down to peer at a small cupboard set in the wall, which she hadn't noticed before. It was locked, of course, but even as she swore out loud with frustration, she remembered the spoons they had used for lunch. Joe hadn't collected their tray, and they were still there on the empty plates. Hurrying back with them, she managed to slide a handle inside the opening and, putting all her strength behind it, she succeeded in forcing the lock.

They stood back, the excitement dying on their faces as they looked at six bottles of tequila and what appeared to be a box of loose bullets. No knife, no gun, nothing that would enable them to gain their release. They were walking back disconsolately into the main room, when she paused, going back again to look at the bottles. Her brain was trying to tell her something . . . but what? She picked up a bottle and stood looking down at it with blind eyes. A weapon . . .? Yes, that was what she had been trying to remember. What she had in her hand was a weapon, but what sort of weapon, for heaven's sake? Well, she could hit Joe over the head with it, of course! She smiled at the thought and swung her arm around in a circle, holding the bottle by its neck.

'Of course!' she exclaimed aloud with an excited laugh as a mental picture of a newsreel she had seen lately flashed through her mind. What she had in her hand was, to all intents and purposes, a *Molotov Cocktail*! Nowadays, rioters filled them with petrol, before setting light to rags stuffed into the necks of uncorked bottles. But hadn't students, during the Hungarian uprising in the nineteen-fifties, used bottles of Vodka in exactly the same way as the modern petrol bomb? Unscrewing the lid she sniffed the raw spirit, tasting a little. Well, it certainly seemed strong enough, but she didn't know about the amount of raw alcohol required for a successful explosion. She hurriedly screwed the cap back on and replaced the bottle as she heard footsteps coming up the stairs.

Ominously, it was Lew. 'The Boss has arrived and wants to see you,' he said, drawing a gun and motioning her to leave the room.

'What . . . what about the boy?' she asked, trying not to let her voice wobble as she felt almost sick and faint with fear.

'He stays here,' Lew said impassively as she bent down to give Carlos a reassuring hug.

'I'll be back soon,' she promised as she was led away, her heart wrenched by Carlos' determined nod and smile, despite the tears which glittered in his dark eyes.

The Boss was indeed here, and obviously in a bad temper. 'I should have guessed that an English nanny would not have been a beautiful young girl!' he said in accusing tone heavily laden with self-disgust. 'Well, Miss Thorne, you certainly fooled me!'

'I . . . I did?' She tried not to look as surprised as she felt.

He held up a copy of the *News*. Even from where she stood, she could see the huge black headlines: FILM STAR KIDNAPPED!

'Sí. It appears that your fiancé, Don Felipe, was in the shop when you were taken by my men. A reporter promptly appeared on the scene and although Don Felipe appears to have been practically incoherent, they soon realised from what he said, that it was his *afianzada*, the film star Marilyn Thorne, who had been kidnapped, together with his nephew Carlos. *Dios!* Now I cannot keep this matter quiet as I would have wished.'

'So, what's the problem, honey?' she said as bravely as she could, finding it easier to act Marilyn's part than that of her own frightened one. 'This way you get two ransoms for the price of one, huh?'

He looked at her startled. 'Ransom? Who said anything about a ransom?'

'But . . . but surely that's why . . . why we've been kidnapped . . .?'

Once again, as yesterday, he threw back his head and roared with laughter. 'You think this is a simple kidnapping? Ah no, alas, my beautiful Miss Thorne. I merely wish my coco to be returned—and to get my hands on Ricardo Diaz,' he added with a vicious snarl.

'Cocoa?' He must be absolutely mad! Her mind spun at the thought of this evil man with a steaming mug of cocoa in his hands! 'What on earth do you want cocoa for?' she asked.

'Coco—cocaine,' he explained, and before he said any more she suddenly understood why he had laughed. Her blood ran cold as she realised that this wasn't a simple matter of kidnapping—a 'pay the money and be rescued' kidnapping. She and Carlos were in the hands of drug pedlars to whom human life, when set beside the unbelievable sums of money involved, meant absolutely nothing.

The man looked at the girl, watching with sardonic amusement as the blood drained from her face. 'Yes, Miss Thorne, cocaine. I run a very successful courier service from the fields where it is grown in Bolivia up to the American border. Ricardo Diaz was a very useful man, a good courier, until he got greedy or suddenly developed a conscience. I haven't yet made up my mind as to the facts, since I haven't seen him lately.' She flinched at the menace in the man's voice.

'However it is, Ricardo has disappeared with a large consignment of the drug and I want it—and him— immediately! That was the message which was delivered to the head of the Costillo family, Don Alvaro, yesterday. I know Don Alvaro to be a hard man, but he is also known for his feelings for his *familia*, yes? I think he will find Ricardo for me.'

'And if he does—you will kill Ricardo?'

The man shrugged. 'Eventually, of course.'

'And if he doesn't, you ... you will kill us?' She received no reply to her question, since the answer was obvious. Continuing to think aloud, she said, 'I . . . I think that even if you find Ricardo, you'll have to . . . to kill us, won't you? We know too much and . . . and we can identify you. So whatever happens, we are dead ducks as far as you are concerned. . . .'

'You are brave, Miss Thorne. I must say that for you. *Si*, you are right. I will be desolated to terminate the existence of someone so lovely, but . . .' he shrugged his shoulders again. 'In the meantime, you may live for a few days. I might need you or the boy to record taped messages to send to Don Alvaro if he should prove to be too slow in his efforts to trace Ricardo. We will see what transpires.' He turned to Lew. 'Take her back,' he commanded, as he turned to leave the room.

'Just a minute,' she said trying to smile at Lew as the sound of the man's car died away. 'Seeing as how I'm not going to live too long, honey, how about letting me have a breath of fresh air? That kid was as sick as a dog last night, and I could do with a gulp of ozone. What do you say?' she asked, trying to control her trembling body.

'The Boss said you was to go upstairs,' he replied stonily.

'Aw, cummon honey! Us Americans ought to be able to come to a little arrangement, huh?' She moved her body sinuously, trying not to look at the box of matches behind him on the table. 'Just a little old peek at God's heaven? That jerk is going to snuff me out like an old candle, honey, and . . . and before I go, I . . . I sure would be grateful to a guy who was nice to me.' She wriggled again as she had seen Marilyn do in her movies. 'Real grateful, if you know what I mean!' she breathed huskily.

Lew gulped. His eyes reflected the sudden thought that he might be able to do more than just look at the film star. Running a finger around his collar which suddenly seemed to be too tight, he shrugged and walked forward to open the door. In a flash she had seized up the box of matches and stuffed them down the front of her dress, moving swiftly forward as he turned.

'Thanks honey,' she murmured, with a suggestive wink. 'You'll never know just how grateful I am going to be. How about coming up and seeing me after supper?'

Oh God! she thought in panic. That sounded more like Mae West than Marilyn! But Lew just gulped again and gave her what he obviously thought was a sexy smile.

'Sure will, sister. What about the kid?'

'No sweat, Lew honey. I'll shove the brat in the toilet. OK?'

'OK ... er ... Marilyn. Like you said, us Americans we ought to ... er ... stick together. Right?'

'Dead right, honey,' she agreed, trying to breath carefully without dislodging the box of matches, and also concentrate on memorising her surroundings as she smiled winsomely up at Lew; whose disgusting leer as he ran his eyes over her body, made her flesh creep.

Back upstairs again with Carlos, she instituted a hive of activity. 'We haven't got long, so we must work very hard and very quickly,' she told him. In some quite extraordinary way she felt excited and exhilarated, despite the sentence of death which had just been pronounced by the evil head of the drugs racket. She and Carlos were going to get out of here, she vowed to herself. If someone had found the message at the gas station, and if Alvaro had been contacted, and if he knew the general direction they had been taken.... It was an awful lot of 'ifs', but he and his men and the police could be scouring the district right now. She had to believe that, *she had to*!

Frantically she and Carlos tore the thin covering of the mattresses, so that the flock insides were ready to use on a fire, finding some bits of paper which they screwed up and hid in the small adjoining room. Rags from the mattress covering were torn into strips and stuffed into the necks of the tequila bottles which Carlos had opened. Even the box of bullets would come in useful, she realised, especially if they were placed on the fire when it started.

At last they were finished. Lyn looked around the room, checking that everything looked as it should. The slit and torn mattresses had been turned over so the mutilation didn't show, and everything else was firmly out of sight.

'OK, Carlos. When I say so, you go and hide in the toilet, OK?' He nodded and she took a deep breath. 'I promise you, darling, if we come out of this unscathed, I will personally hire the best juggler I can find to teach you to toss five balls in the air!'

And then she heard the stairs creak, and the time for action had come. Lyn signalled to Carlos, who disappeared while she waited with baited breath as the footsteps came nearer and nearer. . . .

CHAPTER NINE

LYN's heart was pounding like a sledgehammer as she heard the heavy footsteps on the landing outside the room. Then, as a key turned in the lock, she took a deep breath and switched on a false, brilliant smile as Lew opened the door.

'Come in, honey,' she breathed, walking shakily towards him as her hand slowly undid one of the buttons of her dress; a manoeuvre she had planned beforehand, and one which she hoped would prevent him from looking too carefully around the room. She succeeded beyond her wildest hopes.

'Hell! You sure are really something!' Lew croaked, his eyes firmly riveted to her cleavage. His hands reached out, pulling her roughly against him, the breath forced out of her lungs by his sudden motion, her nostrils filled by the whisky-laden, sour breath fanning her face.

'Hey! Not so fast, honey . . . what's the rush?' she tried to laugh, nearly gagging with nausea at his close proximity as she pushed him away. 'We've got all night!'

'Nope, we ain't.' He pulled her close to him again, although this time she managed to keep her arms free as his hands closed about her slim waist. 'We just had a call from the Boss. That Marquéz, the kid's uncle, he ain't playing the game the way the Boss wants,' Lew muttered, bending her cruelly backwards as he tore open her dress. 'I gotta terminate you, baby . . . but not till later, huh?' he chuckled.

Bending his head to fasten his loathsome lips on to the pale sheen of her exposed breasts, Lew never knew what hit him as, with all the strength at her command, she brought the hard outer edge of her hand in a vicious chopping action down on the back of his exposed neck.

Lyn stepped back as Lew slumped insensibly to the floor, before she felt her gorge rise and she ran for the small toilet, releasing Carlos before she was violently sick.

Splashing her face with cold water, she felt queasy as she fought to control herself. She must proceed with their plan, and as quickly as possible. That ... that dreadful man had been ordered to kill her! She remembered Lew's words ... 'just had a call from the boss'. That also meant there was a telephone in the house—something she hadn't thought about! She went quickly back into the main room to see Carlos looking gingerly down at Lew's body.

'Is he dead, *Tia* Lyn?' Carlos' dark eyes were round with fear.

'No, I just put him to sleep,' she answered as soothingly as she could, quickly doing up the buttons of her dress before bending down to roll Lew over and remove his gun from its holster. 'Quick, Carlos, feel in his pockets to see if he still has that piece of rope he tied my hands up with,' she added, trying to stop the nervous chattering of her teeth.

It had all looked so easy in the films and on television, she thought grimly as she struggled to push Lew's body back on his front, needing the small boy's aid to hold the man's large, calloused hands firm, while she tied them with the rope which had indeed still been in Lew's pocket.

'OK, now help me drag him into the toilet,' she said. It was some time before, panting with the effort, they achieved their objective. She waited until Carlos had gone back into the larger room before she gave Lew, who was beginning to stir, another and even harder blow on the back of his neck. 'I'm not sorry!' she told his prostrate form, her chest heaving with exhaustion. 'You'd have killed me without a thought—and enjoyed it!'

Lyn wasn't too worried about making a noise as she and Carlos made their preparations. Joe downstairs would be expecting some noise from above, since it was unlikely, she thought grimly, that Lew would have kept quiet about his assignation with her that night.

Frantically, she and Carlos turned the mattresses over and she set him to pulling out the dry flock material while she gathered up the crumpled paper and lit a fire in the middle of the room. It seemed to take an age to light, and it was only with an almost superhuman effort that she prevented herself from screaming with frustration. They must hurry—*they must!* Slowly the fire caught, and she patiently fed it small pieces of the mattress stuffing, overjoyed to see how well it was beginning to burn. When she was sure that it wouldn't go out, she tucked Lew's gun into the waistband of her dress and went over to open the door, giving Carlos the key to put in his pocket before sending him up the stairs to wait on the top landing of the three-storied building.

'Now, darling, whatever happens, whatever you hear, you must promise me not to move,' she cautioned him. 'Up you go now, I'll be along in a minute.'

Placing more of the flock material on the fire which was burning well, she seized the box containing the bottles of tequila and ran lightly up the stairs to put them down beside the boy's shivering figure. 'Back soon,' she whispered, before running down and into the room.

The fire wasn't burning fast enough, she realised with a lump of despair, putting on more pieces of the mattresses. If only she had some petrol. . . . Well, it would be a good way of finding out if the alcohol was strong enough to burn she thought, dashing upstairs again for one of the six precious bottles.

Piling on the remains of the mattresses, she emptied the bottle over the fire, and for good measure threw in the bullets which had been in the small cupboard. She was looking frantically about her for something else to burn, when with a *WHOOSH!* the fire ignited into a sheet of flame, sending her stumbling back to the door, almost scorched by the heat. Slipping out of the room, she closed the door carefully behind her and dashed upstairs as quietly as she could.

'What do we do now?' Carlos asked, his body trembling with fear no less than her own.

'We just wait,' she was whispering when with a thunderous, rapid firing effect, the bullets exploded within the room. 'When I tell you to go—when I shout "*run*", I want you to dash down the stairs, not stopping for an instant, through the main room and out of the door. OK? Wait outside the front door for me, and I'll be with you as soon as I can. . . .' She grasped his thin shoulders. 'Are you sure you know what to do?'

'*Sí*,' he nodded.

'Good boy!' She hugged him impulsively. 'Remember—don't stop running until you get out of the front door! I'll be right behind, and. . . .'

'Hey, Lew . . .? Whatcha doing up there, for God's sake?' Joe called up the stairs as yet more bullets exploded loudly behind the closed door.

'Hell, it only needed one bullet to finish off that dame. . . .' Joe grumbled, his heavy shoes thumping on the bare boards as he slowly mounted the stairs. 'Cummon, let's grab the kid and get going,' he called as he reached the landing, and walked towards the door. Lyn's fingers dug warningly into Carlos' shoulders, watching through a crack in the banister as Joe put out his hand to turn the door knob.

By opening the door and providing a fresh current of air, Joe unwittingly provided the fire with all the fuel it needed to become a raging inferno. He staggered back in horror as the sheet of flame met his eyes. 'Oh my Gawd . . .' he yelled. 'Lew . . . Lew, are you OK?' He hesitated for a moment and then raising his arm to shield his face, he plunged into the room.

'Now *run*!' Lyn pushed Carlos down the stairs, praying frantically that he would do what she had told him. She forced herself to wait until she judged that the boy would be outside, her nervous fingers fighting with the small matchsticks as she lit two of the rag wicks stuffed into the necks of the bottles of tequila. As soon as they were safely alight, she picked up the box containing the bottles, and ran lightly down the stairs, past the open door, the fire raging within just a blur as she forged on down the last flight of stairs.

She was halted by a shout as Joe staggered out of the room, his eyes streaming from the smoke as he nevertheless caught a glimpse of her disappearing figure. 'Hey!' he shouted, wrestling to remove his gun and at the same time wipe his eyes.

It was the only chance she was going to get—and she took it. Grabbing a bottle whose wick was burning brightly, she threw it with all her strength at the man who was raising his arm to fire at her. The bottle exploded at his feet, sending him staggering backwards, his gun going off wildly as she threw the second bottle to join the first, before dashing on down towards the main room without a backward glance.

'You . . . you wonderful, wonderful boy!' she panted, fighting to catch her breath as she found Carlos had obeyed her instructions and was waiting for her outside the front door. 'Here, hold these,' she commanded urgently, giving him the box of bottles to hold before forcing herself to go back into the main room. *The telephone!* She must find the telephone before Joe had time to call for reinforcements. It took her two precious minutes before she located the instrument and jerked the wires away from the wall. Rejoining Carlos a moment later, she took his hand and dragged him across the yard towards the entrance to the old mine, which she had spotted when she had persuaded Lew to let her out of the house this afternoon.

Had it only been this afternoon, she thought as they wearily ran up the incline to the mine entrance about two hundred yards away. It seemed as if she had lived through several lifetimes since the departure of Lew and Joe's boss. At the thought of the two men, she looked briefly behind her shoulder, but she could see nothing but a sheet of flame as the window of the small room exploded outwards, the fire clearly taking control. Flames began to lick along the side of the wooden building, the glow being sufficiently bright to light their way towards the entrance to the mine.

Reaching their destination, she and Carlos collapsed in a shuddering heap, completely out of breath and trembling from all they had gone through. Finding a wooden plank to sit on, she forced herself to wait for half an hour, until it was clear that they were safe from pursuit, and that there was apparently no one else in the deserted buildings.

While she waited with her arms about the trembling figure of the boy, she realised that their only safety lay in the fire being seen from a distance. Tomorrow would bring the evil head of the drug smuggling ring, especially if he couldn't get a reply on the telephone. She had no idea where Lew and Joe had been going to take Carlos when they had disposed of her, but clearly the organisation was big enough to pour reinforcements into this place at the first hint of trouble. So, she must burn all the other outbuildings, and create as much of a fire as she could.

Carlos had fallen into a deep, exhausted sleep. With a heavy sigh she made sure that he was as comfortable as possible, before she forced her weary body to retrace her earlier steps; to return and complete the job she had started.

An hour later, Lyn's blackened, grimy figure swayed with dazed weariness as she surveyed the damage she had wrought. All the buildings were blazing merrily, the glow from the fires lighting up the scene as if it were daylight. After some false starts she had found that the best method was to start a small fire, and when it had caught a firm hold, to throw in one of her 'Molotov Cocktails'. The only cataclysmic disaster had been an explosion from one of the buildings, when she realised, far too late, that she had also blown up a car. Luckily she had been on the other side of the yard when the car's gas tank had exploded, it taking her numbed mind some time to comprehend that she had just blown up a method of escape from the deserted mine.

She cursed herself for her folly in not having guessed that their gaolers must have had transport. Weak tears of utter tiredness and exhaustion slid down her smoke-blackened cheeks as she realised they were trapped. If no one saw the flames, they would face extinction tomorrow just as surely as day followed night.

Turning to look back, she saw a scene reminiscent of Dante's Inferno. The combined fires, and especially that of the garage, lit the surrounding countryside for miles around, while the fate of Lew and Joe was too terrible to contemplate with a sane mind. She had carefully avoided looking at the burning main building. She didn't need her conscience to tell her that anyone's murder—even those as wicked and dangerous as Lew and Joe—could never be justified. And she had murdered them just as surely as if she had put a gun to their heads and pulled the trigger. The fact that they would have killed her without blinking an eye proved to be of little comfort, while the prospect of defending herself and the child tomorrow, with the sole aid of a gun she hardly knew how to fire, was too terrible to contemplate. Sinking down beside Carlos' sleeping form, she wound her arms about his warm figure and fell fast asleep.

It seemed only minutes later that she was awakened by the sound of car horns and shouting men. Wearily, she rose to her feet, cautiously peering around the rocky entrance of the mine. Her knees buckled and she almost fainted as she saw, not the boss and his henchmen, but the flashing blue lights on top of what appeared to be a flotilla of police cars!

Hurrying back to shake Carlos awake, she led him out of the mine, her ears full of a strangely familiar, throbbing noise. A helicopter? It couldn't be ... could it? Don't be stupid, she cautioned herself, trying to stifle her wild excitement. The police used helicopters all the time, and why she should possibly imagine that ... Yes! *It was!* It was a red helicopter that was landing in the yard by the burning buildings.

Holding Carlos' hand, she stumbled down the incline, tears of relief streaming from her eyes as she saw Alvaro leap out of the machine and run over to the knot of policemen. It looked, in the flickering firelight, as if they were having to forcefully restrain him from dashing into the burning building, before his shoulders seemed to slump, his tall figure bowed and shaking as he turned away to cover his face with his hands.

Carlos wriggled out of her grip and ran towards his uncle. '*Tio, tio!* Here I am ...!' he shouted. Alvaro whirled at the sound of his voice and cried out with relief as he lifted up the small boy.

A moment later Alvaro raised his head, looking wildly about him until he spied Lyn's still figure standing across the yard. She couldn't move. She was swaying with exhaustion as he put Carlos down and strode towards her, his steps quickening into a run. Crying out with joy, he rushed to clasp her tightly in his arms, his hard, tall body shaking and trembling as much as her own.

'*Oh Dios ... Dios ...!*' he gasped, raining kisses down on her. Gazing up into his face, pale beneath his tan and marked with lines of strain, she saw with wonder that there were tears in his eyes. 'I—I thought you were—were dead,' he whispered. 'I—I thought you had been burnt to death!'

The next few hours seemed to pass by in a series of flickering images which occasionally broke through the cloudy mists of her mental and physical exhaustion. She managed to find the strength to return Carlos' hug before he was led happily away, closely guarded by two of Alvaro's men, to be transported immediately back to where his desperately worried mother waited in Monterrey. She also registered, but did not fully understand, the mixture of admiration and shocked amazement as the crowd of policemen came to understand her part in what had happened; that the entire conflagration and the deaths of the two gangsters was solely due to the efforts of the slight, slim girl with long blonde hair who leant so wearily against Don Alvaro's tall figure.

Lyn reached breaking point when she was taken to the local police station and forced to go through the details of the kidnap over and over again, just in case she had forgotten anything.

'*Señorita! No le oigo bien* ... I cannot hear you,' the regional Chief of Police complained as she sat slumped in her chair.

'I ... I've told you ... told you all I know ...' she was whispering, almost incoherent with fatigue when Alvaro burst in to the small room and angrily demanded her release forthwith—or else he would immediately contact his good friend the Minister of the Interior!

Following his furious interjection, all difficulties magically seemed to melt away and he was allowed to take her back to the helicopter. There, she fell into a deep sleep almost before they took off, not waking until she opened her eyes to find that she was lying in some sort of vehicle and looking up at the familiar white pillars of the entrance to the *hacienda*.

'You ... you've brought me home!' she breathed, turning to the man beside her, weak tears of happiness rolling down her cheeks and making fresh tracks on her grimy skin.

Alvaro gave a low laugh. 'I managed to convince myself that it was the nearest place,' he said, scooping her up in his arms and carrying her through a murmuring crowd of servants, who disappeared at his sharply voiced command.

She gazed up at his tanned face, so close to hers as she felt herself being lowered on to a bed. 'But ... but this isn't my room ...' she muttered, looking about her in puzzlement, her eyes widening as she took in the grandeur of her surroundings, the elegance of the beautiful antiques with which the bedroom was furnished.

'No,' he agreed, smiling over his shoulder as he walked towards a door. 'It's mine,' he added, disappearing from view, only to reappear some moments later in a red silk dressing gown. Moving across to open an en suite bathroom door, she heard the sound of water running and then he was back, standing beside the bed and looking down at her with such an expression of tenderness in his eyes that her breath seemed to be caught in her throat.

Speechless, her eyes still glazed and shadowed with the experiences of the last two days, she made no protest as he started to remove her filthy smoke-filled clothes, his hands so tender and gentle that his touch brought fresh tears to her eyes. As if from a distance she heard Alvaro swear gratingly under his breath, the blood draining from his face as he gazed down at the livid bruises on her pale skin, caused by her journey in the van.

'It . . . it's all right,' she whispered. 'They don't hurt very much.'

He swore again, clasping her naked body tightly to his, before gently lifting her up and carrying her through into the bathroom. She was vaguely aware of a large room, that looked like an elaborate film set: a large square jacuzzi bath, floor to ceiling mirrors reflecting gold fittings and a deep, cream carpet over which he moved towards a glass walled section of the room containing a shower.

There must be enough room for ten people in here, she thought bemusedly as he set her gently down, swiftly removing his silk gown before joining her in the cubicle and closing the glass doors.

Lyn had no more than a fleeting glance of his naked figure, before he deftly moved her beneath the cascading water and briskly began to wash her long blonde hair.

The fatigue seemed to wash out of her as under his expert administrations she shed all the smoke and grime of her recent experiences. The soft feel of a soapy sponge as he rhythmically stroked every inch of her body, had no sexual connotations and was hypnotically soothing, Lyn thought, standing quiescent until he was satisfied that he had removed every last trace of dirt. Moving under his guidance like an automoton, she let him wrap her hair in a small towel before he gathered a larger one and proceeded to dry her with slow, gentle movements.

Wrapped warmly in one of his silk gowns she was carried silently in his arms back to the bedroom. 'It is time for you to sleep,' he murmured, lowering her to the bed.

'Alvaro, please . . . please don't leave me!' she breathed, terrified of being left alone in the dark and possessed by an overwhelming need to have him beside her.

'*Ah, querida,*' his lips parted in a slow, warm smile. 'Where else should I sleep but in my own bed, hmm?' he murmured as he lay down beside her, lowering his head to seek the delicate pulse throbbing at the base of her throat.

Lyn caught her breath as a shaft of pure pleasure shivered down her skin, following the downward path of his mouth as it moved to encompass the fresh warm curve of her breast.

'You must sleep now,' he said as she instinctively moved her body in innocent provocation against his, a small moan of disappointment issuing from her lips.

'Must I . . . must I sleep?' she whispered, twining her arms about his neck.

'Yes, my passionate little one, I'm afraid you must!' he answered firmly, the underlying low note of tender amusement in his voice as he gathered her into the warmth and security of his body, being the last thing she heard as she dutifully obeyed his commands and drifted away into oblivion.

Shafts of morning sunlight streamed in through the open windows, falling on the figure of the girl lying in the big double bed. You really ought to get up! Lyn told herself sternly. Fancy being still in bed at . . . she turned to look at Alvaro's bedside clock . . . at half past ten. It was quite disgraceful! She laughed aloud with sheer happiness as she continued to lie back on the pillows, stretching her satiated, languorous body, her cheeks blushing as she recalled the previous long night of passion. She had been back here at the *hacienda* for two days now, and apart from the occasional excursions into some of the other rooms in the house, Alvaro had kept her closely confined to this room, the bed and . . . and within his arms!

As commanded by him, she had indeed slept deeply following her rescue, only waking late the next morning in a cold sweat from a nightmare, relieved to find Alvaro's concerned face leaning over her, replacing the dreadful, ghostly image of Lew.

'It is all right, *querida* . . .' he said slowly and gently as he put a cool hand on her fevered brow.

'Oh, I . . . I had this terrible dream . . .' she gasped. 'I . . . I was alone in that room in the house, and there was fire everywhere . . . everywhere. And then there he was with a gun in his hand!' she gabbled fearfully as traces of the dream returned to cloud her mind. 'I shouted to him to go away, I knew he was dead, I knew I'd killed him . . . but he kept coming nearer and nearer . . .'

'Ah, my darling,' he drew her trembling body into his warm arms. 'It is all over now. They were bad, evil men, who had caused the death of many people. You cannot blame yourself for ridding the world of such vermin— *never*!'

It was such a relief to relax in his embrace, to hear the reassuring thud of Alvaro's heart as he clasped her tightly to his chest. If only she could stay within the safe haven of his arms for the rest of her life, breathing in the warm, musky scent of his body and knowing that his strength would hold at bay the nightmare which had tormented her.

Gradually, as her mind broke free of her dream, she realised that the rough hairs on his chest were brushing the tips of her breasts, and she felt the muscles of the long, warm length of his body against hers, his hands gently stroking the soft skin of her back in a soothing motion. His actions were having the opposite effect to what he intended, she thought in bemusement as a fire seemed to be kindled low in her loins which swiftly spread to encompass her whole being. She trembled, pressing herself closer as she swiftly became mindless to all else but her need of him.

'Ah, my sweet little one,' he softly protested. 'After such—such terrible experiences, you must rest . . .'

Despite his words, his body's arousal betrayed him, his arms tightening about her and his frame shaking in reaction to her sensual, erotic movements against him.

'Love me . . .' she breathed. 'Please, just love me . . .' She no longer cared if she exposed her feelings for him, driven by a force, an intensity of passion that cried out for his possession.

'Dios!' he groaned. 'I should not—and yet, how can I resist your sweetness, my passionate little virgin . . .?' she barely caught the softly murmured words before his lips closed over hers in a kiss that sent waves of heat pulsating through her body.

His lovemaking was exquisitely gentle, tenderness mingling with strength and mastery as he carefully paced her pleasure with his own. He seemed to instinctively know that he was helping to banish for ever all the scars and mental torture of the past days, tenderly leading her to an ecstatically prolonged climax before allowing her to slip down into a deep, fathomless sleep, tightly wrapped in the total security of his arms.

She had been awoken by his light touch on her shoulder, and she sat up against the pillows as he placed a tray on her lap, containing a bowl of soup and some warm, crusty bread.

She hadn't realised just how hungry she was, and gratefully began to sip the hot liquid as Alvaro filled in the background to the kidnapping and her rescue.

'I have just been talking to Felipe on the telephone. It appears that the police had no trouble, following your and Carlos' description of the head of the drug ring, in rounding him up. So you need have no fear now, *querida*, he is safely behind bars.'

'How . . . how did you find us so quickly?' she asked, her white teeth tearing into the bread—she didn't think she had ever tasted anything quite so delicious.

'From the message you and Carlos left on the door of the toilet at the gas station. What a clever girl you are . . .'

'. . . So you did find it!'

Alvaro laughed. '*Por Dios!* That message is going to cost me a small fortune! I had no idea so many women . . . er . . . used public conveniences quite so often. I must have had hundreds of telephone calls! However, darling girl, I am so delighted at your safe return, that it seems only right they should all have a reward, hmm?'

'Yes, well . . .' Lyn blushed as he reached forward and gently removed a crumb lodged between her breasts which, the sheet having slipped down, were now fully exposed to his view.

'Ah no,' he murmured as she tried to cover herself. 'That is how I like to see you, *amada*, the sight of your lovely body gives me much pleasure.'

She blushed again as his hands slowly caressed her taut breasts, a languid torpor invading her limbs at the sensuous touch of his fingers. She made no demur as he removed the tray and gently drew back the sheet to feast his eyes on her body.

'*Dios!* How could a man tire of wanting one such as you . . .?' he breathed thickly as desire flooded her veins, hotly tempestuous and demanding her sweet surrender. She gasped and moaned as his lovemaking became more roughly sensual and demanding than ever before, taking complete possession of her senses. She felt herself drowning in an avalanche of passion as he brought her to fulfilment, crying out as great shudders ran through her slim frame.

Lyn sighed with pleasure at memories of Alvaro's lovemaking and looked again at the time. It was now eleven o'clock and she really *must* get up! Although they had spent most of the past days in bed, Alvaro had also found the time to be in constant contact with his office, and his home in Monterrey. She had been immensely relieved when he had told her that the police had closed the case as far as Lew and Joe's deaths were concerned. 'The building caught fire and they perished,' Alvaro had said firmly. 'That is the official statement and no one wishes to dispute it, especially not the police who are delighted at your resourcefulness. But I have been told to express the sympathy and regrets of the police chief at having to interrogate you so roughly. Although, he hopes you won't tell anyone about the petrol bomb effect of tequila bottles!'

It seemed that Carlos had completely recovered from his ordeal and Felipe and Doña Elena had also got over the shock, spending most of their time comforting his distraught mother. 'They are, of course, profoundly grateful to you for all you did,' Alvaro had said. 'And send much love. My mother, especially, insists that you stay up here and fully regain your strength. No,' he had added with a sad shake of his head, 'we have received no word yet of Ricardo's whereabouts, I'm afraid. Of course the police will want to talk to him. What he did was very wicked, *no*?'

He had heard nothing further, until a call had come through late last night. Alvaro had refused to tell her any more, other than that he had to go to Mexico City and would be back just as soon as he could. 'The matter may take some days, so be patient, my little one, hmm?' he had laughed as she hugged him, filled with a mindless dread at being left on her own. 'You will hear from me soon, I promise you,' he had assured her before leaving at dawn.

Lyn had slipped out of bed and was wrapping herself in Alvaro's large robe, when she heard a knock on the door. It must be Maria with her morning cup of coffee, she realised, since Alvaro had forbidden the other servants to approach this end of the house. Although how he could possibly imagine that they didn't know of her presence . . .

'Good morning, Lyn.'

She looked up startled, her eyes widening in

astonishment as she saw Dolores' slim tall figure standing in the doorway.

'I have ordered a pot of coffee for us both. I hope you don't mind?'

Lyn stared at the cool, elegant woman, completely unable to say anything. A tide of deep crimson covered her face as Dolores' black eyes swept expressively over Lyn's figure in Alvaro's dressing gown and the crumpled sheets on the bed.

'What . . . what are you doing here?' Lyn managed to say at last.

'To see you dear, of course.' Dolores' smile was surprisingly friendly, although Lyn noticed that it didn't quite reach her dark, unfathomable eyes.

'Why did you want to see me?'

'So many questions!' Dolores trilled as Maria brought in a tray containing a pot of coffee and two cups. 'Shall I be mother?' she asked brightly, not waiting for an answer as she began to pour the coffee.

At the unusual spectacle of Dolores being so pleasant, cold steel bands began to tighten about Lyn's heart.

'Of course I'm always pleased to see you, Lyn, but in this case I . . . er . . . I was asked to come.' Dolores flashed her another smile. 'I told Alvaro that you might find it embarrassing,' she shrugged, 'but he seemed to think that you would understand.'

'OK, let's cut the cackle,' Lyn said huskily, suddenly feeling sick. 'Why have you come to see me, and what will I find embarrassing, but about which I am clearly supposed to be understanding.'

'Now dear, there's no need to sound so bitter.' Dolores smiled again.

'I think I'm about to find out that there is,' Lyn retorted grimly. 'I suggest that you say what you have to, drink up your coffee, and then get out!'

'Oh dear!' The older woman looked at her with pity.

'I knew this wouldn't be easy. I'm here with some clothes for you to wear, to tell you just how grateful the family are for all you have done and to give you a plane ticket for your flight back to America—preferably on an aeroplane leaving today.'

'That's all?'

'Well, no, not ... er ... not quite. Alvaro has also given me a letter for you. I must say that you're quite different from his usual type of little girl,' she said, handing Lyn a plain, sealed envelope. 'I'm really surprised at the way he's behaved this time. He's usually so very careful not to involve me or his family in his little escapades. He's been very naughty.' She shook her head sorrowfully.

Lyn's body seemed filled with mindless panic. 'If ... if you're trying to say that Alvaro is trying to get rid of me, I ... I don't believe you,' she cried defiantly, looking at Dolores with loathing. 'He couldn't do this to me!'

'Couldn't he dear? Well I can assure you he has! However, why don't you read your letter and then, if you are such a glutton for punishment, you can telephone him. He should be in his plane by now, about half way between Monterrey and Mexico City. He can receive calls, and I'm sure he will tell you in words far more brutal than mine, exactly how he views the situation. Don't let me stand in your way, dear!'

All the fight went out of Lyn at Dolores' confident words. Feeling nauseous she dashed for the bathroom, slamming the door shut behind her and resting her fevered brow on the cool mirrored surface. Taking a deep breath, she opened the envelope which was still tightly clutched in her hands, trying to focus her dazed eyes on the firm angular black writing which completely covered the piece of paper, and which didn't even begin with a salutation.

'It has been a pleasant idyll, my dear, but what has been between us must now cease. You have your life to lead and so do I and while I am deeply grateful for all your kindness to my family, I must insist that we see each other no more than is strictly necessary. Any attempt to seek to change my mind would be a fruitless effort on your part.

Alvaro'

Gasping with pain, it was a long time before Lyn could face going back into the bedroom. How Alvaro could be doing this to her, she had no idea, except that he was. Numbly she walked across the cream carpet and opened the door.

'If you'll give me the clothes you've brought, I'll . . . I'll get dressed,' she said with listless apathy.

'Of course,' Dolores agreed quickly. 'There's a plane that leaves this afternoon . . .' She put the clothes on a chair and hurried out of the room.

Lyn sank down on the bed, burying her face in Alvaro's pillow, her nostrils filled with the lingering scent of his cologne. Great shudders began to shake her slim body as she wept as if her heart were broken—which indeed, for all intents and purposes, it was.

CHAPTER TEN

THE mourners filed slowly past Lyn, many of them murmuring words of comfort while others, like some old members of the circus, just clasped her wordlessly in their arms. Of course, reason told her that it was four years since Uncle Charley had retired from the nomadic life, but they seemed to find it almost as incredible as she did that Charley Harris would no longer be able to dress in his red coat, cracking his whip in the centre of the circus ring.

'OK, Miss Lyn, if you're ready?' Sunk in thought, Lyn hadn't realised that she was standing alone on the bottom step of the church, the cars bearing the last of the mourners disappearing down the dusty road. With a sad sigh she turned to see Rusty, her uncle's young foreman.

'Yes, I'm ready to go back home,' she said, following him to the ranch pick-up. Although, just how long she could call it home, she wasn't too sure. Her uncle had needed round-the-clock nursing for this last month since she had returned from Mexico, and by the time she had paid the medical bills as well as the funeral expenses, there would be virtually nothing left to pay next month's wages for the ranch hands. She had to keep them on if she was to continue breeding the Arab horses that had been her uncle's life, and it was no good thinking she could top up the necessary money from her stunt work. The accident in Mexico seemed to have given her a fear of heights, which meant that she could no longer do much of her work, even if she felt she could face going back into the film world, which God knows she didn't. Her last, searing experience at the

169

hands of Larry Wilde had been enough to last anyone a lifetime, she thought grimly. Her perilous financial position was the reason why she had allowed her uncle's attorney to pressure her into meeting a possible purchaser for the property.

'You really don't have a choice, Miss Harris,' he had pointed out dryly, well aware of her situation. 'I have been assured by the agent acting for the purchaser that the gentleman concerned will continue to run the place as it always has been, and also keep on the men. It's a very fair offer, and I think that you ought to at least think about accepting it—you may not do as well later.'

'I expect you know just how much we're all going to miss your uncle, Miss Lyn,' Rusty was saying. 'I was just a young boy, fresh out of school when he took me on, and I ain't wanting to work anywhere's else.'

'I know, Rusty. I . . . I've never had any other real home than the ranch, either. I'll do what I can, you know that.'

'Sure I do,' he murmured sympathetically. 'All I wanted to say was that me and the boys, well, we don't need cash that urgently, if you get my drift. We can rub along OK—until you manage to get yourself straight, that is.'

'Oh, Rusty . . .' her eyes filled with tears and she hunted for her handkerchief to blow her nose furiously. 'I do . . . do appreciate what you've said, and I'll try and do what's best for you all. You never know,' she added, trying to be cheerful, 'something might turn up.'

'Yeah, bound to,' he agreed, her heart quailing at his cheerful optimism. 'Well, here we are,' he announced as he brought the pick-up to a halt outside the long, low ranchhouse.

'Thank you for taking me to the church,' she said, getting down from the vehicle.

'Least I could do. Are you sure you're OK? Me and the boys, we kinda thought we'd go into town and have a quiet drink in the saloon. Sort of to remember your uncle, you know? But if you'd like me to stick around . . .'

'No, I'm fine,' Lyn said as cheerfully as she could, not able to face telling him that she was due to meet a prospective purchaser for the ranch in an hour's time. 'And . . . and thank you for being so kind and helpful,' she added reaching up to peck him on the cheek.

Rusty's face blushed a brick red. 'Yeah . . . well, I'll see you around,' he called as he drove away in a cloud of dust.

Taking a deep breath, she forced herself to walk into the empty house which seemed so lonely without her uncle's large, cheerful presence. The man who wanted to buy the ranch wouldn't be here for an hour, so she had plenty of time to take off her black dress and have a shower. It would be getting dark by the time he arrived, of course, but he might like to have a look around, and jeans and a shirt would be better than this figure-hugging dress and the high-heeled shoes to which she was so unaccustomed.

Standing beneath the warm needle-spray of the shower, she set about lathering every square inch of her skin with determined resolution, as though by doing so she could cleanse away all her troubles, past and present. The last month had been sheer hell, she thought dismally. Uncle Charley had grown weaker each succeeding day, and on top of having to watch someone she loved just wasting away, there had been the ever-present dull throbbing heartache of her own to contend with. She had heard somewhere that time was a great healer, but she knew better! A month might not seem very long, but in terms of seconds, minutes and hours it was a lifetime. Sitting beside her uncle for long silent stretches, with nothing to fill her mind but her memories of the all-too-few magical days spent with Alvaro, she despaired of ever being able to forget his strong, magnetic personality.

She couldn't fool herself, of course. She had known from the start of their relationship, even when they had snarled and fenced so bitterly with each other, that she must be wary of getting involved with a man like Alvaro. Such a dynamically forceful man was way outside her league, and telling herself that she wasn't able to resist him and that she was desperately in love, hadn't solved anything, had it? He had taken all she had to give: her virginity and her love, while in return, he had never even told her that he loved her. So how could she have expected their affair to lead to anything but heartbreak?

You know what you are, don't you? she told herself roughly. Not only are you a fool, but you're a sad object lesson for any girl stupid enough to be swayed by the sins of the flesh! Lyn gave a bitter laugh which sounded oddly muffled by the cascading water. 'The sins of the flesh' was a good old biblical phrase, and really very apt when she came to think about it in relation to the brief affair between herself and Alvaro. She had always known that he was a man who just took what he wanted. As it had turned out, it was Lyn whom he had wanted, but she had also known that such a man was capable of being equally callous in discarding the object of his previous affections, just as soon as he was bored or found a new amusement. And that was exactly what had happened, wasn't it? Only . . . only she wasn't made of the same finely tempered steel as Alvaro. She hadn't been able to recover so easily, in fact, she hadn't been able to recover at all. She still felt every bit as devastated by his desertion as she had on that day well over a month ago. . . .

Her thoughts were interrupted by the loud sound of the door bell. It couldn't possibly be the prospective purchaser of the ranch, it was much too early, she thought, stepping out of the shower and wrapping a towel around her slim figure. It must be Rusty with a message he had forgotten to give her during the earlier part of the day—not surprising really when they had been so involved with the funeral. . . .

Lyn padded across her bedroom, hearing the bell ring again. 'I'm coming, Rusty, hang on . . .' she called, moving down the hall. 'What have you forgotten this time?' she said, taking off her shower cap as she opened the door. 'I bet that . . . *A-A-Alvaro* . . .!'

'Good afternoon, my dear Lyn. Or should it be "good evening"?' he asked in a cool voice, casually consulting his watch.

'W-what . . . what are you d-doing here . . .?' she whispered, clinging for dear life to the heavy oak front door as she felt her knees buckle beneath her. Her dazed eyes tried to focus on the tall, elegant figure dressed as always in the forefront of male fashion. No one has a right to be so good looking, she thought in despair, viewing his handsome tanned face and sweep of black hair curling over the collar of his dark grey formal suit.

Still reeling from the shock of his sudden reappearance in her life, she watched dumbly as he moved smoothly past her trembling figure into the hall and looked about him with interest.

'What . . . what are you doing here? What do you want?' she croaked hoarsely.

'So welcoming . . .!' he murmured cynically. 'I may say, my dear Lyn, that you look as charming as ever, even if you are wearing . . . er . . . rather more than when I last saw you,' he added blandly.

'For God's sake!' Lyn's face flushed as she clutched the towel tightly to her naked figure, seething with indignation at the sight of the man who had caused her the unhappiest month of her life, casually strolling on through into the sitting room as if he owned the place.

'What in the hell do you think you're doing here? No

one gave you permission to come waltzing into my house and . . . and. . . .'

'Oh yes they did—your attorney for one.'

'My . . . my attorney?'

'And my own curiosity, of course,' he drawled.

'Curiosity . . .?'

'My dear Lyn, must you echo my every word?' he murmured, lifting one dark eyebrow in sardonic mockery.

Her eyes swept over his powerful frame and it was with the utmost difficulty that she held on to her temper. Apart from anything else, she was at a severe disadvantage standing here in the sitting room, her body still wet from the shower and only covered by a towel.

'I . . . I must ask you to leave immediately,' she said with as much dignity as she could muster. 'I have to see someone very soon, and. . . .'

'I know. That is precisely why I am here,' he replied in the same, maddening bland voice as he sat down in a comfortable chair.

'You mean . . .?' she gazed at him open-mouthed, almost rigid with shock.

'I mean that I have made your attorney an offer. One which he tells me you are prepared to consider. Yes,' he added, looking about him, 'this is a very pleasant room.'

'What absolute nonsense!' she snorted with disbelief. 'You cannot have the slightest interest in buying this small ranch, so why have you come here? Slumming, I suppose,' she added, her voice dripping with contempt.

'Oh, I wouldn't say that,' he replied, coolly as he took out his heavy gold case, selecting and lighting a cheroot with unhurried calm movements.

'No—I bet you wouldn't! Nevertheless, for someone as rich as yourself, this is just a little down the financial ladder, isn't it? Or do you get your kicks from seeing how the other half live?' She gestured about her at the comfortable but somewhat shabby furniture.

She gained considerable satisfaction from noticing the flush of colour beneath his tanned face and a muscle beating furiously in his tightening jaw. However, he seemed to be impervious to her taunts, remaining as cold as ice and fully in control of himself.

'I did mention that I was curious, didn't I? By the way, if you want to change or slip into something more revealing—please don't let me stop you!' he purred silkily. 'My mother, by the way, is every bit as curious as I am.'

'Your mother is worth ten of you!' she snapped. 'Although why she, or you for that matter, should be so consumed by curiosity, I have no idea!'

'Well, I must admit that I was anxious to see just what it was about this place that made it so very much more ... er ... more attractive than anything I had to offer,' he drawled, a slight humourless smile twisting his lips.

'*What you had to offer?* Hah! If I hadn't just come back from my uncle's funeral, I'd laugh in your face!' she cried. 'What you had to offer, was nothing! Less than nothing, if I remember correctly—and believe me, I do!'

'Is that really the sort of woman you are? That you would spit in my face when I had laid my world at your feet? I could not believe it—and yet—*Por Dios!* I see it is so!' He rose menacingly from the chair, his sheer height and the breadth of his shoulders seeming to make the room seem suddenly too small.

'I only wish I had been given the opportunity of spitting at you,' she ground out angrily. 'But you made very certain that I didn't. The great Don Alvaro—my God, you're pathetic! Laying your world at my feet ...?' she laughed wildly. 'That's rich, that is! Well, let me tell you, that I regard your so-called "offer" as nothing but the ... the deepest insult I've ever had the misfortune to receive!'

'You consider yourself insulted, señorita?' His eyes flashed with a terrible fury as he moved slowly towards her. 'Tell me, I would be fascinated to know, what is it that a man can give you, before you don't feel insulted, hmm?'

She backed nervously away from his threatening figure. 'I ... I want you to leave this house. Go away! Go away and never ... never come back!' she cried, running swiftly past him out of the room, down the corridor and into the sanctuary of her bedroom. She was leaning against the closed door, panting and trying to catch her breath, when she found herself suddenly catapulted across the room as with one blow from his foot he smashed the door open and advanced into the bedroom.

'Get out!' she screamed, as with slow deliberation Alvaro removed his jacket and tie, before throwing them on to a chair, all the while conducting an unwavering, analytical appraisal of the slim blonde girl holding the towel so tightly about her body, whose large blue eyes flashed with anger as his dark hooded gaze travelled insolently over her trembling figure.

'I will go,' he purred quietly as he moved slowly towards her. 'I will go when I have received the answer I require. What is it that you want, eh? You have made it very clear that you do not want anything that I can offer you, so tell me—just what does a *puta* like you desire, hmm?'

'Don't you dare call me that!' she yelled, shaking with such fury and outrage that without a thought her hand flew to his face. The next second she cried out with pain as a stinging blow caught her own cheek, the force of the slap sending her tumbling back on to her bed.

'You ... you hit me!' Lyn gasped, lifting a trembling

hand to her face, almost unable to believe what was happening to her.

'*Cristos!* I have never struck a woman before in my life!' he hissed. '*Por Dios*—the Good Lord knows you have driven me to it!' He was breathing heavily, the eyes beneath their heavy lids darkening as he gazed down at the sprawled figure of the girl on the bed, her long blonde hair a shining mass about her pale face.

'I once called you a . . . a cream puff,' she retorted breathlessly, struggling to sit up. 'And that's just what you are! A grown man of your age and experience— hiding behind a woman's skirts the way you did. . . .'

'*Basta! Silencio!*' he thundered, catching hold of her foot and swiftly whipping her figure over so that she lay face down on the bed cover. Before she had time to even draw a breath, let alone express her furious disgust at his behaviour, she felt the weight of his body on the bed beside her.

Her screams were muffled as with humiliating ease he ripped the towel away from her struggling figure. She had never fought anyone so hard in all her life, using her hands and feet to hit any part of his body that she could reach, but her puny efforts were of no avail against his overwhelming strength, which was lent an extra force by his raging fury. At last she lay exhausted, her naked body racked by deep sobs which shook her slim frame as he quickly stripped off his clothes. Through her tears, she saw him advance towards her and cried out in fear.

'*No!* No—*you can't*! It . . . it's rape . . .!'

'You told me, the night we first made love, that all you felt for me was lust,' he snarled menacingly. 'So, *querida*, if you would like to tell me the difference between what you felt then, and what I feel now, I would be pleased to hear it!'

'You . . . you're terribly wrong,' she cried. 'It was you who . . .'

'. . . you protest too late, my little one,' he retorted thickly, catching hold of her wildly gesticulating hands and pinning them above her head, while his other hand fastened determinedly on the soft fullness of one breast, his thumb slowly circling her nipple and sparking off an explosion deep in her stomach that caused her to moan helplessly.

'Is that how you groan for your lover, hmm?' he goaded as his head bent to take the place of his hand, his action sending shuddering waves pulsating through her body.

'I . . . I've never had . . . had any lover but you. You . . . you know that . . .!' she cried wildly, struggling to tear her hands away from his firm grasp.

'Who is the man you left me for? *Tell me!*' he demanded roughly, holding her body firmly beneath him as he stared down intently into the blue eyes swimming with tears.

'No one! I . . .' Her trembling protest was smothered by the crushing force of his lips, her heart pounding with the pain and pleasure of his tongue as he savagely forced her lips apart, ravaging the inner sweetness of her mouth. The blood soared in her veins as feelings she had tried to repress rose up to mock her earlier defiance. Her flesh melted beneath the feel of his hands on her body, and the humiliating realisation that despite everything he had said and done, she still needed and could not live without him.

'Tell me his name!' Alvaro hissed through clenched teeth, but she could only shake her head helplessly as his anger mounted to an uncontrollable pitch, the potent force of his raw masculinity raging unchecked. He swore harshly against the softness of her mouth, his breathing ragged and uneven as his hands and lips became cruel instruments of torture.

'Very well! Before I have finished with you, you will be begging me for release, pleading for the merciful deliverance that only *my* possession can assuage. You are my woman, and it will be my name that is on your lips, *my body* that you crave!'

Lyn thought that she would never survive what followed: an exquisite torture of the senses as he led her to the very brink of sensual, erotic ecstasy, caressing every tender, secret place until she moaned and cried out helplessly for physical release—all to no avail. Not until she was writhing beneath him like some wild creature, endlessly repeating his name in a mindless, shuddering refrain, did he pause for a moment from the demanding arousal of his mouth and hands, studying the sweet curves of her breasts and the warm, sinuous line of her thighs. With a deep, despairing groan he parted her legs and possessed her with a raging, thrusting urgency, producing an explosion of such magnitude that she almost fainted.

She returned to full consciousness to find herself locked in Alvaro's arms, his warm lips gently kissing away the tears from her eyes.

'I—I cannot ask for your forgiveness, because there is no way I can even forgive myself . . .' he whispered, the dampness in his eyes matching hers as he tenderly brushed the hair from her perspiring brow. '*Mi preciosa, mi amada.* Oh, my dearest little one, I have been in such torture! Even if you felt nothing for me, how could you be so cruel as to leave me with no word from your own lips? Just a message that you were returning to your lover, and that you never wished to see me again? *Cristos!*' he groaned deeply. 'I thought I would surely die when I heard that. The return of my letter of love and offer of marriage—just torn into little pieces . . . *Jesús*, I was in such despair!'

Lyn gazed up at the strained lines in his face not able to clearly comprehend what she was hearing. 'But . . . but you left me. You s-sent m-me that terrible, cold letter saying . . . saying that we must part. . . .' She gasped as the tears continued to roll down her cheeks in a steady stream.

'*Ah no!* Holy mother of God—how could I have done such a thing as you say?' With infinite tenderness he gently wiped away her tears. 'That I, who loved and wished to marry you, whose dreams have been haunted by the memory of your sweet virginal cries of pleasure at our lovemaking, *mi bella amada*, that I should say I wished us to part. . . . It is not possible!'

'You . . . you love me?' Lyn whispered uncertainly, not able to fully accept what she was hearing.

'How could you have ever doubted it, my dearest love? Although I, myself, did not fully understand what was happening to me when I stood in that small hospital, watching a sleeping girl as the day lengthened into evening. I did not understand why I felt such a deep rage against you and my brother—why I felt physically ill at the thought that you were a woman who had known many men. . . .'

'. . . but I hadn't! I. . . .'

'Hush, little one, let me finish, hmm? Let me try to explain why I became such a—a monster, so wickedly cruel and unkind to you. You must understand that I did not know what was happening to me, I—I couldn't seem to leave you alone and I was secretly pleased to obey my stepmother's instructions because that meant you would be in my power, and that was important to me. I wished to cause you pain—the pain that I felt in not possessing you. And then your sweet image invaded my every waking moment, even my dreams—*Dios!* I thought I would go mad! It was only when I held you in my arms by the waterfall that the scales fell from my eyes and I realised that I loved you—totally and completely!'

His arms tightened about her trembling figure as he gave a deep sigh. 'Can you imagine how I felt? You were engaged to my own dear brother who was younger than I and looked to me for guidance. And yet—and yet there I was wanting his *afianzada* with such a fierce longing—only the Good Lord knows how hard I tried to fight to destroy that love. The nights of torment . . .!'

Lyn wound her slim arms about his dark head. 'Oh, Alvaro . . . I love you so much . . .' she murmured softly against his tanned cheek.

'. . . I could hardly control myself, and then I nearly raped you when the bull. . . . *What did you just say?*' he demanded roughly, suddenly rolling over on top of her body and staring intently down into her face. Lyn looked up at the man she loved, and without whom life had no meaning for her. It didn't seem to matter any more about the tumultuous anger which had sparked between them, the confused disaster of her departure from Mexico. Now, as his hard, firm body pinned her to the bed, nothing seemed to matter beside the glorious, almost unbelievable fact that he loved her every bit as much as she loved him.

'I . . . I said that I love you. I love you with all my heart and have done for a long, long time,' she murmured quietly.

'Dios!' he breathed, still not really believing what she said. 'But that night—that night we first made love, you told me that you merely felt lust. . . .'

'No! No!' she protested. 'I thought that was what *you* felt. I—I was already so . . . so much in love that I. . . .' she blushed and smiled shyly at him. 'I wanted you to make love to me so much, that I tried not to think that what I was doing was wrong. Making love to a man who . . . who just wanted my body. . . .' she whispered.

He smothered a groan. 'I was so confused that night. Suddenly, it appeared that you weren't Marilyn, not the fiancée of my brother and I was free to possess you. I did not know of your love, but I wanted you so much, I yearned so fiercely to possess your lovely body . . . with love and reverence, you understand. You were so loving, so warm and responsive. . . .' He kissed her passionately. 'I could hardly contain myself. I was determined to ask you to marry me the next day and then. . . .' His body began to shake at the memory of her kidnapping.

'You will never know! Those two, terrible days I went through the torture of the damned. I knew, as soon as I received that evil man's message that there was little chance for your life—or for my nephew. To have found at last the woman with whom I wished to spend the rest of my life, only to have you cruelly torn from my arms. . . .' He lay back on the bed, his powerful frame shuddering as he recalled the strain of waiting for some news of her, his mounting despair as the hours had crept by.

'I—I couldn't talk to Felipe, he had gone completely to pieces; Mercedes was in a similar way, naturally. Only with my mother could I let myself go. I—I think I even cried when I told her about you and how much I loved you. She was so understanding, so kind. She told me that she had known straight away, when you came to the *hacienda*, that you were the one for me. She said she was sure that you loved me, even if you did not realise it, and that I must give you time and be very, very gentle when—and if—you were rescued.'

He gathered her lovingly into his arms. 'When we found you alive, I thought I would die of joy, but I tried to remember the terrible things you had been through, and my mother's words. I wanted to declare my deep love, but I hesitated, and then when I had to go to Mexico City, I—I took a chance and before catching my plane, I sat down and wrote all I felt for you, my darling. How I wished us to be married, and how I would love and cherish you all my life. I—I thought a letter would give you time to think while I was away . . . I never—I never imagined . . .' he groaned deeply.

'When Felipe gave me your message, I nearly killed him!'

'*Felipe?*' Lyn struggled to sit up, her blue eyes wide with shock. 'I never saw Felipe! All I ever had was that cruel letter from you.'

'*Querida*—I have already told you that I sent you no "cruel" letter. I merely expressed all my love, all my devotion. . . .'

'But . . . but . . . this is crazy! What's more—I . . . I can prove what I've been saying,' she told him earnestly, rolling out of his arms to open a drawer in the bedside table. 'Here,' she said, handing him the creased, tear-stained piece of paper. 'See for yourself. See why I . . . I left Mexico as soon as I could.'

She watched as with a puzzled look he took the letter from her hand, noting how his face darkened with fury, his hands trembling with anger as he read the brief words. 'Who gave you this!' he whispered savagely. 'I did not write this to you—*Por Dios!*' he swore loudly. 'I will kill whoever did such a terrible thing.'

'But you did send it,' she protested. 'You sent Dolores with a plane ticket, some clothes, and . . . and that letter.'

'No, no, no—I did not! Dolores? I gave my letter to Felipe. . . .' he paused, running his hand distractedly through his hair, before clicking his fingers. 'Marilyn—of course!' He rolled over to pick up her bedside phone. 'Operator? I wish to call Spain . . .'

'You . . . you can't just ring Spain! It might be the middle of the night, for heaven's sake, and why Spain?' she demanded, totally confused.

He put his hand over the receiver. 'While we were up at the *hacienda*—I kept you there, not only to make love, but to avoid all the newspaper reporters camping outside our house. Marilyn managed to inveigle her way into the house, wearing a quite terrible black wig. She had seen the reports of your kidnap and rescue, and

I imagine she wanted to know what was going on. All I knew was that when I flew down, that day I was going to Mexico City, she and Felipe were cooing like doves, declaring their intention of getting married and preparing to call a press conference—which I immediately cancelled. I understood the plan was for her to state that she had been recuperating with my family when "she" was kidnapped!'

His face creased into a wide smile, his shoulders shaking with amusement. '*Dios!*—that woman is amazing!' He turned to the phone. 'Yes, I wish to call Madrid. . . .' He rattled off a number before leaning back on the pillows to wait for his call to come through.

'Well, what could I do?' he laughed. 'I could only agree to let Felipe marry his Marilyn, yes? They are on honeymoon in Spain right now, and she tells me that she is to retire from the film world and concentrate on being a good wife.'

Lyn smiled with delight. 'I'm so glad. I'm sure that she really does love your brother very much, and isn't just after his money as you thought.'

He nodded. 'I wasn't sure, but when she told myself and Felipe about her previous marriage, and why she had asked you to masquerade on her behalf, I saw that if she loved him enough to tell us that, their marriage would be a success.'

'I—I couldn't tell you about her. I'd promised, you see. . . .'

'I understand my precious one. I also know all about *you*!' His powerful shoulders shook with amusement. '*Dios!* I never thought I would be going to marry a bareback circus rider—I must be *loco!*'

'You haven't asked me yet . . .' she murmured, glancing up at him through her eyelashes.

'Ah, beloved—in a moment. . . .' he replied, turning to speak rapidly into the telephone. '*Che, Felipe . . .? Muchas gracias . . .!*' he said a few minutes later. 'Give my love to Marilyn. *Si, Si.* All is well. Yes. . . .' he grinned at Lyn. 'Yes, maybe if I go down on my knees, she might agree to marry me. I live in hope! *Adios*!' he added, replacing the receiver.

'Marilyn sends you much love.' He leaned over to take her in his arms and kiss her passionately. 'It is thanks to her pleading, together with that of my mother, that I am here. I was so stiff with hurt pride, so terribly wounded by your desertion. But Marilyn said you were a kind, sweet girl—which you are—and she begged me to come and see you. To hear from your own lips that you did not love me.' He sighed deeply. 'How right she was.'

'But you still haven't told me what really happened about that letter. It is your handwriting, isn't it?'

'Yes.' He paused for a moment and then took a deep breath. 'It is true that I . . . er . . . I and Dolores we. . . .'

'. . . you were lovers? It's all right, Alvaro I know that,' she said quietly.

He flushed slightly beneath his tan. 'I—I am thirty-five years of age, my darling, and I'm afraid I have been no monk. However, from the moment I saw you in the hospital, no one else has existed for me—no one! I trust that you will believe me on this, because it is important that you know that I had a long talk with Dolores the morning after you first arrived at the *hacienda*. I told her I was terminating our . . . er . . . our affair. Unfortunately, she did not seem to accept my decision, and so I had to write her a very plain letter. It is the second page of that letter that she gave you.'

'I still don't understand?' Lyn looked at him in total confusion.

'How could you understand such a wicked woman, hmm?' he murmured, drawing her closer to him. 'But you must understand what happened. When I flew down to Monterrey that morning, the house was in confusion. I couldn't tell you at the time—you had been through too much already—but Ricardo's body had been found in Mexico City. He had been killed by accomplices in the drug ring who found him before I did.'

'Oh no!' Lyn trembled in his arms. 'Poor Carlos and Mercedes!'

'Yes, it is very bad. My sister is slowly recovering, but . . . we will talk about it all later, yes? On that day, Marilyn had turned up and Felipe was so overjoyed that he hardly knew what he was doing. I handed him my letter for delivery to you, and flew off to Mexico City to identify the body, after telling everyone, in my joy and happiness, that I wished to marry you. Dolores had arrived to comfort my mother, and Felipe tells me that she offered to take the letter up to you at the *hacienda*. Felipe on cloud nine, handed it over to her and thought no more about it. My phone call just now was to ask him what he had done with my letter—something I never thought to ask before.'

'So, Dolores. . . . She took your letter out of the envelope and substituted that piece of paper, which you had sent her some weeks before? But . . . but she was so definite, Alvaro. She said I could phone you in your plane if I wanted to hear the truth from you.'

'Yes,' he sighed deeply. 'It was clearly a risk she took, but one that nearly came off. Although how, in God's name, she thought I would ever turn back to her when I had known you—it is a mystery.'

'Well, she's very . . . very attractive,' Lyn said in a small voice.

Mentally consigning Dolores to the devil, and quite determined that the evil woman, who had caused his beloved Lyn such heartache, would find herself living many hundreds of miles from Monterrey by the time they returned there, Alvaro clasped Lyn tightly in his arms.

'I love you,' he said slowly. 'I have loved you from

the first moment I saw you. I love your purity and innocence and I have found within your arms something I have never experienced with any other woman—a truly mystical blending of mind and body.' His voice became thick and husky, his hands sensually caressing her soft skin. 'You have become my whole life, my entire existence, *mi adorada*, and if I don't marry you very soon,' he added in a husky murmur, 'I will shoot myself!'

'Oh, Alvaro . . .' she breathed ecstatically, before looking at him, her eyes clouded with concern. 'What am I going to do with this ranch?'

'I was never interested in your ranch,' he said impatiently. 'Only in you. Sell it, give it away, keep it— who cares!'

'But . . . but what about the men?' she gasped as his fingers stroked her full, warm breasts, the tips swollen with desire.

'My dearest love,' he breathed thickly, his touch becoming more pressing, more intimate. 'Do what you will. If they like horses, bring them and the animals down with you to my *estancia*—anything you like. But, *por Dios*, Lyn! Please say that you will marry me?'

Lyn gazed dreamily up into his smiling, handsome face, the dark hooded eyes gleaming down at her with overwhelming desire and love. 'Oh yes! Yes please, Alvaro. . . .'

His name was lost beneath the fierce possession of his lips as she melted so willingly and pliantly beneath him. She had, she realised, found her true home at last, locked safely within the haven of Alvaro's tender embrace.

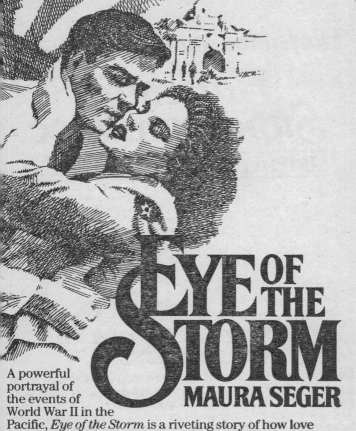

EYE OF THE STORM

MAURA SEGER

A powerful portrayal of the events of World War II in the Pacific, *Eye of the Storm* is a riveting story of how love triumphs over hatred. Aboard a ship steaming toward Corregidor, Army Lt. Maggie Lawrence meets Marine Sgt. Anthony Gargano. Despite military regulations against fraternization, they resolve to face together whatever lies ahead. ... A searing novel by the author named by *Romantic Times* as 1984's Most Versatile Romance Author.

Take these 4 best-selling novels FREE

Harlequin Presents...

Take these
4 best-selling novels
FREE

Yes! Four sophisticated,
contemporary love stories
by four world-famous
authors of romance
FREE, as your
introduction to the Harlequin Presents
subscription plan. Thrill to **Anne Mather**'s
passionate story BORN OUT OF LOVE, set
in the Caribbean.... Travel to darkest Africa
in **Violet Winspear**'s TIME OF THE TEMPTRESS....Let
Charlotte Lamb take you to the fascinating world of London's
Fleet Street in MAN'S WORLD.... Discover beautiful Greece in
Sally Wentworth's moving romance SAY HELLO TO YESTERDAY.

Join the millions of avid Harlequin readers all over the
world who delight in the magic of a really exciting novel.
EIGHT great NEW titles published EACH MONTH!
Each month you will get to know exciting, interesting,
true-to-life people .... You'll be swept to distant lands you've
dreamed of visiting .... Intrigue, adventure, romance, and
the destiny of many lives will thrill you through each
Harlequin Presents novel.

FREE Gift Certificate
and subscription reservation

Mail this coupon today!

Harlequin Reader Service

In the U.S.A.
2504 West Southern Ave.
Tempe, AZ 85282

In Canada
P.O. Box 2800, Postal Station A
5170 Yonge Street,
Willowdale, Ont. M2N 6J3

Please send me my 4 Harlequin Presents books free. Also, reserve a subscription to the 8 new Harlequin Presents novels published each month. Each month I will receive 8 new Presents novels at the low price of $1.75 each [*Total— $14.00 a month*]. There are no shipping and handling or any other hidden charges. I am free to cancel at any time, but even if I do, these first 4 books are still mine to keep absolutely FREE without any obligation. **108 BPP CAHE**

NAME   (PLEASE PRINT)

ADDRESS   APT. NO.

CITY

STATE/PROV.   ZIP/POSTAL CODE